DEATH ON THE TURNING TIDE

Nick Shaw jumps at the chance to explore the island of Jersey for his job as a travel writer. Accompanying him is his journalist friend Ben Ryland, who wants to follow up a story about modern-day smuggling that could be his big break. Disregarding the risks, Ryland hares off to probe further into a suspicious death — only to vanish without a trace. Searching for him, Shaw is inexorably drawn into the world of smuggling — where the wrong move can lead to a watery grave . . .

KATHERINE HUTTON

DEATH ON THE TURNING TIDE

Complete and Unabridged

LINFORD
Leicester

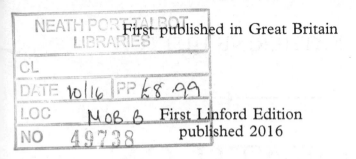

First published in Great Britain

First Linford Edition
published 2016

A catalogue record for this book is available
from the British Library.

ISBN 978–1–4448–3022–4

Published by
F. A. Thorpe (Publishing)
Anstey, Leicestershire

Set by Words & Graphics Ltd.
Anstey, Leicestershire
Printed and bound in Great Britain by
T. J. International Ltd., Padstow, Cornwall

This book is printed on acid-free paper

1

The horizon dipped down as the ferry rose on the crest of a wave, and Nick Shaw battled with his nausea. Sitting rigidly on one of the outside seats, he checked his watch once again, silently willing the hands to move faster and deliver him to dry land, but there was still over an hour left before they were due to reach Jersey.

He normally had no trouble on boats, and had been looking forward to the journey, but a far-too-late and far-too-indulgent night out had conspired with the windy weather to give him a bout of seasickness he would not forget in a hurry. At least the cold air was helping, as was the bottle of ginger ale his friend, Benedict Ryland, had brought out for him.

To Shaw's annoyance, Ryland's hangover had actually improved from being at sea, and he was inside, eating and reading with perfect composure.

'I can see you're suffering a bit.'

Shaw looked round and saw an old man, his mackintosh tightly wrapped and belted around him, peering at him quizzically.

'It's a bit rougher than I'd like it to be.'

'You can't do much sailing, then. This is fine compared to some of the crossings I've had!' The man sat opposite Shaw and smiled broadly.

'There was one time,' he went on, 'a couple of years ago this October, which got even me a bit worried. It was a force seven gale when we left Poole Harbour — the captain really shouldn't have set out at all — and after only half an hour the whole ship was rearing like a bucking bronco.

'One poor woman who had been trying to get to the loo fell and broke her ankle so badly they had to get the helicopter out to her.'

'What, at sea?' Shaw asked, incredulously.

'Yes, and the gale was even worse by then.' The man nodded gleefully. 'I could

2

hear the helicopter for ages as they tried to winch her up safely. Managed it in the end, but I thought the whole lot of them would end up in the sea a few times.

'Then, once they were away back to the mainland, the tannoy kept announcing number plates: *Will the owner of registration number OV10 NHT please come to the hold* kind of thing. Turned out the cars were crashing around into each other like kids' toys; and, being a crossing to Jersey, those weren't just Ford Fiestas and the like — they were BMWs, Mercedes, Porsches ... I tell you, the insurance claims won't have been pretty.

'By the time we got to St Helier, half the passengers were filling out complaint forms; and the other half were positively grey, having run out of food to throw up.'

'It must have been a nightmarish four hours!' Shaw said, wondering how he would have coped with such a journey.

'Closer to eight!' the man said with a hint of triumph. 'One of the engines had packed up, so it could only go at half-speed.'

'Bloody hell!' Shaw exclaimed, and

then began to laugh. 'Well, it does put my discomfort into some perspective, I suppose.'

'That's right. This is just a bit dippy. Nothing to worry about. You're not missing much by being out here anyway. In a while, you'll get a lovely view of Guernsey as we get closer. Are you stopping there or going on to Jersey?'

'Jersey,' Shaw confirmed. 'My friend and I are spending a week there.'

The old man nodded approvingly. 'You can see a lot in a week. Would you like a few recommendations?'

Shaw had in fact researched the island in some detail already. He was a travel writer and intended to work up a few articles to help pay for the trip. It never hurt to find out what someone else thought worth seeing, though. He took another sip of ginger ale.

'I'm not going anywhere until we dock, and it'll take my mind off the swell; so, if you're happy to talk, I'm very happy to listen.'

★ ★ ★

The entrance to the Port of Jersey brought a welcome end to the crossing. Shaw's newfound friend had been amusing and informative, but the arrival on dry land was still a relief.

He and Ryland shouldered their rucksacks and set off to search for their hotel.

It had been Ryland who had first put forward the idea of a trip to Jersey. He was a journalist Shaw had met through his own dealings with newspapers a few years ago, and they had kept in touch.

Ryland specialised in investigative reporting on a minor scale, and had recently become interested in how smuggling persisted in island communities. After some research on the Devon coast, he had become convinced that most coastlines still maintained a trade in various illicit substances.

Shaw had expressed a certain degree of scepticism, but liked the idea of a visit to Jersey, which he had never been to. His girlfriend, Detective Sergeant Louisa West, was busy working on a lengthy case and had no idea when she would be able to take any leave, so he had readily accepted Ryland's proposal.

'How are you feeling now?' Ryland asked.

'Grim, but nothing that a good night's sleep won't fix. It's not far to the *Pomme d'Or*. It's right on Liberation Square.'

The short walk did much to restore Shaw's stomach, and the warm July sun was freshened by the sea breeze. It was the first visit to Jersey — or any of the Channel Islands — for both of them, and their initial impressions were extremely positive.

For Shaw, the pleasure he felt at exploring a new location was quickly overcoming his seasickness, and he began to mentally map out his surroundings. He was good with conventional maps, but also had an almost photographic memory for towns if he had the chance to walk around them.

Ten minutes after disembarking, they reached the *Pomme d'Or* hotel, and were soon relaxing in the lounge with a drink — a soft drink, in Shaw's case.

'I thought we could start tomorrow with a walk round St Helier; do the castle, see about hiring a car?' Ryland suggested.

'Sounds all right to me. We can get some information for you about the coast at the tourist office, and I'll pick up a bus timetable for myself.'

'I'd like to get the lie of the land a bit before I head off to find a story, so we can do some of the tourist stuff together if you like,' Ryland said. 'I'd be interested in seeing the War Tunnels.'

'Well, I've got a long list of places I want to visit; so when you're off interrogating bootleggers and dodgy fishermen, I can do the things you're not so keen on,' Shaw said, pulling a notebook out of his pocket.

'Let's get another round in, and we can work through that list. Do you feel up to a proper drink yet?' Ryland raised an eyebrow and smiled lopsidedly.

It was a smile that had worked well on informants and barmaids alike over the years.

Shaw considered the condition of his

stomach, and judged it safe to risk a shot of whisky.

A short while later, they had divided up the island's attractions into the ones they would check out on their own and those they would go to together.

'And that's the lot!' Ryland said with satisfaction. 'Whether we get through it all is another matter, of course. If I get a lead, I'll have to leave you to it.'

'I very much doubt that you'll ferret out anything much here. Not in a week,' Shaw replied.

'Then I'll just have a holiday, won't I? But don't be so defeatist, you never know. Anyway, I'm hungry, and there's supposed to be a seriously good steak restaurant round the corner.'

Ryland drained his glass, and the two of them walked out into the evening sunshine.

A minute later, a man who had been sitting a little way off in the hotel's lobby unhurriedly folded his newspaper and left the hotel.

★ ★ ★

Shaw woke the next morning with renewed energy, and over breakfast he talked animatedly about the island's attractions with Ryland. By half-past nine they were ready to set out on a walk round St Helier. It was going to be a hot day and the sun was already warm.

Shaw stretched with sheer pleasure at the feel of the sun and the smell of the sea.

Ryland watched him with amusement. 'You're in a good mood today,' he observed.

'Why not? I've got a whole island to explore, brilliant weather to do it in, and I can make some money out of it later on.'

'When you put it like that . . . ' Ryland conceded.

'Exactly. Now, I want to take the ferry out to Elizabeth Castle first of all.'

'A ferry? I thought it was part of the island.'

'It is, but the castle is on a tidal island,' Shaw replied, setting out along the street. 'When the tide is out you can walk along the causeway but look at the sea now.' He gestured to the harbour where the boats were almost at their highest.

'Unless you want to swim, we need to get one of the castle ferries; although they're really a kind of bus-boat hybrid. I think they're affectionately known as 'puddleducks'.'

Ryland raised an eyebrow. 'I've ridden in some strange vehicles in my time, but never a duck.'

'There's a first time for everything, Ben,' Shaw said. 'Come on, the castle's supposed to be good, and I want to get round it in time to come back to the centre for lunch.'

He walked briskly to the ferry and they boarded the strange vehicle, whereupon it trundled through the water to the castle.

Elizabeth Castle was well worth the visit, and Shaw took pictures and made notes while Ryland went along for the ride, checking his phone several times for messages.

After an hour and a half, they had seen the exhibitions, caught some of the tour, and were just waiting to see the midday parade. Leaning with his back against a parapet, Shaw began mentally going through the list of places he intended to check out in St Helier. A barely audible sound made him open his eyes. Ryland's mobile had chirruped, and the journalist quickly took it from his pocket and opened the message.

'Finally!' Ryland said, and began a call to the sender. 'Rick? Hi, it's Ben. What have you got for me?' He wandered a little way off as he usually did. Shaw had noticed several times that Ryland never really liked standing still. A few minutes later, he finished the call and walked back with an excited gleam in his eye.

'Good news?' Shaw asked.

'Could be. Rick's found me a possible contact — an old coastguard,' Ryland replied, looking pleased with himself.

'I have to admit, if anyone should know about smuggling, it's the coastguards. Who's Rick, by the way?'

'A freelance researcher. I've used him a few times when I was too busy to do all the background on a story. Apparently this guy, George Bisson, is willing to meet me tomorrow if I can go out to his house. Rick says he sounded very keen to pass on what he called 'some suspicions with a lifetime's experience to back them up'. I'll have to leave the zoo to you, and pick up a car either tonight or tomorrow morning.' Ryland slapped Shaw cheerfully on the back. 'See! I told you I'd get somewhere.'

'Unless, of course, your contact turns out to be a first-class fantasist, or a chancer who thinks he can cadge a few beers off a gullible journalist.'

Ryland laughed. 'That's only happened a couple of times. You're just worried you'll look weird going to the zoo on your own.'

'You know me too well.' Shaw checked his watch. 'They should be starting the parade any time now. We'd better go down to the courtyard.'

They descended from the old fort to the parade ground in the seventeenth-century section of the castle, and were in time to see a group of conscripted tourists being put through their paces before helping to fire a cannon.

Shaw and Ryland walked back across the causeway, now uncovered in the low tide, and headed into the pedestrianised area of St Helier.

Over lunch, Ryland talked animatedly about his hopes for a newsworthy story about modern smuggling.

'I've been listening to people along the Dorset coast, people who know what really goes on, and the word is that there's a very professional group who claim they can smuggle pretty much anything into the country. The police have managed to shut down a couple of routes, but never got any of the top guys. There's a rumour that a lot of the contraband was coming from mainland Europe via the Channel Islands.'

'I don't know how they can hope to prevent smuggling if it's done cleverly,' Shaw said, frowning at the thought. 'There must be so many places where you can bring a boat close enough to a cove or beach to row to shore.'

'Exactly! That's what makes it so difficult. If you come into the country by plane or via the Channel Tunnel, both you and your luggage get checked; but arriving from the sea is a different matter entirely.' Ryland's face was slightly flushed and his excitement was obvious. 'The first the police know of it is when the drugs or cigarettes or whatever appear on the streets. By then, the smugglers are long gone — but there must be a pattern to it, or the dealers wouldn't be able to meet the demand. It's big business, and a lot of the time the profits go to fund more serious crimes.'

'But, realistically, Ben, do you think you'll be able to find enough out for a big story?' Shaw could not help expressing his scepticism. Ryland often had grand ideas, and although he had been lucky a couple of times, his bread and butter was normally fairly standard news.

'You'll just have to wait and see, Nick.' Ryland leaned back, smiling secretively.

'Fair enough,' Shaw said, with a slightly exasperated tone. 'Let's get the bill, and then we can have a wander round the centre before we find you a car to hire. I want to get it today so we can drive out to a pub I think you'll appreciate for supper.'

'You're the travel expert.' Ryland

readily acquiesced and they spent the afternoon looking round St Helier.

★   ★   ★

With Shaw leading, they went in and out of the bustling streets, noting the high-end shops and kitsch tourist traps alike. Shaw took endless photographs and made notes in his usual way. With only a week on the island, he would not have time to start writing anything up, and he was not sure what angle he was going to take yet. It was better to have too much material to work with rather than too little.

Ryland understood the need for proper research better than most of Shaw's friends, and seemed content to trail along with him, offering the odd comment on a shop or a monument; but even he started to tire after a couple of hours. 'Time for a break,' he announced firmly as a clock somewhere out of sight struck four. 'It's getting physically painful walking past tea shops and pubs. Besides, I have an idea that could help both of us.' He steered

Shaw to the nearest café, and ordered coffee and cake, before leaving with a cry of: 'I'll be back in a minute.'

Shaw realised that his feet were aching too, and the battery on his camera was low. He resisted the urge to flick through his photographs; there might be something later he would want to record, and it was pointless running the battery down further. Instead, he looked through his notes and started on his own coffee.

Ryland returned a few minutes later with two copies of the *Jersey Evening Post*. 'There you go! I always start with the local papers when I visit somewhere new. Drink your coffee, eat something, and have a read.'

'Good thinking, Ben,' Shaw said, taking one of the papers. 'You kept going pretty well though. When Louisa comes on my orientation walks she usually gives up far sooner.'

'I would have thought she'd be pretty fit, being in the force.'

'She is. Part of her complaint is that I don't walk fast enough for her,' Shaw admitted.

They sat in companionable silence for a while, reading the newspapers.

Shaw had just found a section written in the local dialect of *Jèrriais* when Ryland let out an exclamation. Putting his paper down, Shaw asked: 'What is it?'

Ryland spread out the page he had been reading and jabbed a finger at a small article, barely two inches long. 'Read that,' he said.

' "Local businessman found dead",' Shaw read out. 'What's the significance, Ben?'

'The dead man was Harry Scadden. Apparently his body was found yesterday in a barn on his land.' Ryland looked excited and troubled in about equal measure. 'The thing is, his name came up a few times when I was researching in Dorset. Several of the people I talked to believe that he's connected with the smuggling ring here.'

'Do you think his death is linked to what you're hoping to investigate?' Shaw asked.

'It might well be,' Ryland said. 'He was found hanged, and it could have been suicide — but, reading between the lines, I don't think the police have ruled out foul play.' He folded the newspaper. 'There's competition in smuggling, just like any business; but unlike most, the rivals don't just undercut each other. Scadden could have been killed to make way for someone else.'

'You'd better talk to the police then.'

'Yes, they might have some information,' Ryland mused.

'I meant, you should tell them what you know.'

'I will! But sometimes there can be a little give-and-take, you know. I've liaised with the police before. Of course, there may be no connection. Maybe the guy had incurable cancer or something, and decided to end it himself. I've known it to happen — but it could also be much more important than that.'

Ryland drained his cup. 'Come on. I want to fix up a car. Things are happening, Nick! I can't afford to laze around.'

'Okay,' Shaw said, stuffed the last of his cake into his mouth and followed Ryland as he strode out. A moment later, he hurried back in, and apologetically paid the bill.

★　★　★

The evening sunshine was still hot as Ryland drove them west, following Shaw's instructions. It was not a long journey, though the roads grew increasingly narrow when they turned south, away from the main route.

'We're going to run out of road soon, Nick. I hope you know where you're taking us,' Ryland said, drawing over to let a car coming the other way edge past them.

'Just a bit further. Have faith,' Shaw replied, the map on his lap. 'It should be just round this corner . . . yes! There it is.'

'Oh, I see. Okay, very fitting, I suppose,' Ryland said, glancing at the pub sign for The Smuggler's Inn. 'Looks like there's a car park over there.' So saying, he swung the car round, wheels crunching on the gravel, and they got out.

The hamlet that included The Smuggler's Inn was at the eastern end of a bay that swept away from them enticingly. The tide was coming in, but they could see that the sand was soft and golden; a pathway led west towards a rocky hill that ran out to meet the sea.

There was a light breeze and a scent of the sea that Shaw found almost intoxicating. 'What do you think?' he said, gesturing at the view.

'Damn near perfect,' Ryland replied appreciatively. 'Only needs a pint of beer to complete the scene; and as there's a pub right here, I think we can sort that out.'

After a good meal and a brief chat with the landlady about the pub's history, they wandered outside and leant against the wall that separated the beach from the car park.

'The tide's right in now,' Ryland observed, shading his eyes from the setting sun. 'You can see just how tempting a place this would have been for smugglers in the old days. Slide a boat in here at night, get the goods unloaded, and to hell with the Customs Men. Rum, lace, tea ... you name it. It was a real industry.'

He took a gulp from the bottle of beer he had brought out with him.

'Did you know that Guernsey was actually allowed, by Royal Charter, to smuggle until sometime in the eighteenth century? They could quite legally buy from Europe and sell to the British smugglers. Even after the crackdown, these islands made a lot of money that way.'

'And some people still do?' Shaw asked, staring out at the sea.

'You bet your life they do, and it's a lot more harmful stuff than tea these days.'

Back at the hotel, they agreed to go their separate ways the following day — Shaw to test out the public transport and visit the zoo, and Ryland to chase up his lead.

'Night, Ben. Good luck with your coastguard. Tell me all about it when you buy dinner tomorrow.'

'What!'

'You're working now, right? You can put it on your expenses as entertaining.' Shaw grinned at the look on Ryland's face and left for bed. He reflected that if Ryland really was on to something, it would do him good. He had seemed restless for a couple of months.

Shaw's own work was far less stressful, and he was beginning to make a name for himself as a witty and accurate guide to hotels, destinations and holiday experiences. The money was sporadic but sufficient, and he was able to do the thing he loved most of all — travel. The thought of being tied down to the never-ending work that people like Ryland did, however exciting he knew it could be, just did not appeal to him.

As he reached his room, his thoughts turned to Louisa. She too enjoyed the pressure of her job, most of the time, and the energy she had could be contagious. Smiling to himself, he set up his laptop, and turned his attention to planning a special trip for her next birthday.

★ ★ ★

A few miles away, on the north-east coast, the last rays of the setting sun were reflecting off the sea — frustratingly, right onto George Bisson's binoculars.

He shifted his position slightly, trying to get a better angle. The notebook by his side had the names of many boats and times written in it, with a few of the entries underlined. His small cottage was on a slight promontory, and the view that had taken his fancy twenty-three years ago was now the focus of his obsession.

Since retiring early from the Jersey Coastguards due to ill health, he had continued to watch the seas, determined to prove he had been right.

A sailing boat rounded the headland, and his eyes flicked automatically down to the name on its side — *Spirit of the Wind*. He relaxed. That one belonged to Jacob Guerrien and was only ever used for pleasure trips with family and friends.

Guerrien liked to sail all afternoon and into the evening, only returning when the light failed. Bisson had been out with him a few times himself.

He lowered the binoculars and rubbed

his eyes. He was torn between his desire to continue his vigil, and the tiredness that was causing his eyes to droop. His medication did its job, but the side-effects took their toll, and he wanted to be on the ball for meeting the reporter tomorrow. It seemed unlikely the man would be of much use, but there was a chance that he could be more open-minded than the others.

He decided to call it a day, reluctantly admitting to himself that it probably would not make any difference if he was keeping watch or not; there was only so much he could do on his own.

Setting his binoculars back on the windowsill, Bisson eased himself into his favourite armchair and picked up the *Jersey Evening Post*. Flicking idly through the pages, he stopped abruptly.

His heart began to race. *Harry Scadden dead! What the hell does that mean?* He shook his head in confusion. This did not fit his theory at all, and it probably meant that he would have to bring all his plans forward.

He put the paper down, pulled himself

painfully out of the chair, and picked up his telephone. It was time for the first test of his dubious alliance with Harland; and, given the contempt he felt for the man, he rather wished it would be his last. After a few rings, Harland picked up, and Bisson got straight to the point.

'Have you seen the paper, about Scadden?'

'Yes. Interesting isn't it?' Harland replied and Bisson could imagine the slight smile that no doubt accompanied the voice.

'Bloody inconvenient, I'd have said!' Bisson retorted. 'Can you nose around and find out what happened? It might be nothing to do with us, but if there *is* a connection, I think we should know.'

'Couldn't agree more, George,' Harland said, pronouncing the name in the French way that always annoyed Bisson. 'I'll see what I can find out.'

He paused, and Bisson was about to put the phone down when Harland spoke again. 'I don't suppose it was you, was it? You didn't go off the deep end again, did you?'

His voice was as smooth as engine oil, and the upward lilt of the words teased Bisson intolerably.

'No, it bloody wasn't!' Bisson shouted and slammed down the phone. Breathing heavily, he moved to the window once more. Scadden's death was problematic, although he could not deny that personally it was satisfying to know the bastard was gone.

The breeze had grown stiffer as darkness fell, and he could hear the spray hitting the rocks below his garden. *What way is the wind blowing now?* he wondered, gazing out to sea.

2

Sitting in the bus station, Shaw jotted a few notes about the café he had found for breakfast and how it compared to the much more expensive fare at the hotel. He was heading off on his own to try out the public transport, which consisted of buses radiating out from the central bus station in St Helier.

He and Ryland had another night booked at the *Pomme d'Or*, and would then be looking for guesthouses for the other five nights in order to see more of the island. While they were still based in the town, Shaw wanted to make use of the buses as much as possible, and had decided to try out the route that would take him to the Durrell Wildlife Park — the island's famous zoo.

From there, he would catch another bus that took him round a section of the east of Jersey. He would also like to get to the Neolithic site *La Hougue Bie* when possible. If Ryland was going to be too taken up with working, then Shaw would get another car for himself — good though the buses seemed, it would be a lot quicker and more flexible if he had his own transport.

He looked up from his notebook, his mind turning to Ryland. It was strange that this Harry Scadden had died just before they arrived on the island; perhaps this time Ryland really was on to something. He was a risk-taker, and had nearly lost his job last year, working on a story that turned out to be too much rumour and not enough evidence. Shaw had never known quite what it was all about, and Ryland had been unusually tight-lipped about it.

Banishing both Ryland and smuggling from his thoughts for the moment, Shaw caught his bus and had a productive morning. The zoo was every bit as good as he had heard, and the buses were prompt and not too crowded.

He then headed towards the east coast and Mont Orgueil Castle. As the bus drew up in Gorey, he caught his first glimpse of the castle, a towering stone fortress that dominated the village and seashore.

He stopped to take some photographs, then decided to buy a sandwich to eat on a bench overlooking the harbour. He picked up a drink and the local paper, strolled to his seat, and began to eat.

He had finished his lunch and educated himself about the local football teams before he flipped the paper over and flicked briefly through the news. A familiar name caught his eye and he turned back, smoothed the paper flat, and started reading. Harry Scadden, it appeared, might not have taken his own life, but have been helped along. The details were sketchy, but it was obvious to Shaw that the police were on the hunt for a murderer.

He started to feel a slight twinge of unease. If Scadden's death was indeed linked with the smuggling ring, then was Ryland really equipped to investigate?

He leaned back on the wooden bench, his eyes resting on the castle. It was only a few months ago that he had been confronted by violent death for the first time in his life. He and Louisa had found a body, pierced by arrows, and had been drawn into the police investigation: she through her job, and he through circumstance. The image of the dead man, one eye ruined by an arrow shaft, was still clear in his memory, and he had no wish to repeat the experience.

Looking once more at the article, Shaw noted that Scadden had lived in the parish of St Martin when he was on Jersey, but owned property in France as well. Very handy if Ryland's suspicions were founded, he thought. There was no mention of family, or of who had discovered the body, which was unusual; but there might be reasons why the police were holding back some of the information.

Finally, he removed the sheet with the article on it and folded it up to put in the small rucksack he had brought with him. Ryland had probably already seen it, but he might be too busy with Bisson to have picked up the paper. He had been going to see the police early in the morning to 'exchange information', as he had put it, before meeting the ex-coastguard.

Shaw sent a brief text, asking: *Any luck?*

Shouldering his bag, he then set off to tackle the climb up to the castle; glad that he was reasonably fit, as the approach from Gorey harbour was steep. He arrived at the Castle panting.

Inside were yet more steps to be negotiated as he explored the exhibits and views. Stopping once again for breath at the highest point that could be reached, he stared at the blue sea and could just make out the coast of France — or convinced himself he could. His phone buzzed and he took it out.

Ryland had replied with: *Possibly. Where are you?*

Shaw texted back that he was in Gorey and a minute later his phone rang. 'Hello?'

'Nick, I'm pretty nearby in St Catherine's. Do you want to meet up, or would that upset your schedule?'

Shaw thought for a moment. He was due to catch another bus back to St

Helier in an hour's time, but it would not hurt to change that. 'Okay. Can you find the front entrance to Mont Orgueil Castle?'

'No problem. I should be there in about fifteen minutes at the most.'

'I may be a bit longer myself, but I'll see you at the entrance soon.' Shaw rang off.

Ryland had sounded distracted, but Shaw decided it was probably excitement if he was getting somewhere. Taking one last shot of the panoramic view, he descended to the lower levels, and eventually left the castle.

He saw Ryland from quite a way off: a lean, self-confident figure resting against the car with sunglasses on, basking in the sunshine. He smiled as Shaw approached.

'Nice old place, this. Good view of the sea.'

'And of the boats coming from France I expect,' Shaw answered with a questioning look.

Ryland took off his dark glasses and nodded. 'That did come to mind,' he agreed. 'According to Mr Bisson, there's a lot going on here that the tourists don't notice.'

He looked up at the flags waving from the top of the castle. 'You know, the police think Scadden was murdered.'

Shaw nodded. 'There was a hint of that in this morning's paper. I wondered if you'd seen it.'

'I have, but that's not how I know. I went along to the station earlier and left a statement detailing the rumours I'd heard about Harry Scadden. They were being very tight-lipped about it, but I overheard a couple of officers talking, and it sounds like there are inconsistencies with the hanging. I also got the impression that my information about Scadden's activities was a confirmation of something they already had suspicions about.'

'You're not likely to have to wait around while they investigate, then?' Shaw asked.

'Don't think so, which is handy. I've only got this week off work. They'd understand, under the circumstances, but it will be a lot easier all round if I can leave when you do.' Ryland opened the car door.

'I want to check something out, and I can fill you in on George Bisson's ideas if you like.'

'Where are we going?' Shaw said as they turned onto the coastal road.

'North,' Ryland replied laconically, then added: 'I'll tell you in a bit.'

Shaw waited for Ryland to elaborate, realising that his friend was ordering his thoughts before relating them. They drove for a few minutes in silence.

Finally, Ryland began. 'George Bisson was a coastguard for thirty years, give or take. Loved the job, all aspects of it; from the dramatic rescues to the day-to-day tasks of maintaining the boats, advising sailors, all that kind of stuff. There used to be a Mrs Bisson, but I gather she died a few years ago. George carried on with his work, and would have continued until normal retirement age, but he had to leave early due to ill health.

'He was a bit cagey about that, actually. He fell during a rescue at sea and got his leg trapped between his boat and the one that was taking on water. He walks with a very pronounced limp; you can see why he wouldn't be able to do active duty, or whatever it's called in the coastguards, but I think there was something else behind it as well.'

He stopped talking as they came to a junction and waited for a large tractor to bump around the turning.

'What kind of something else?' Shaw prompted when they moved off again.

'Well, he says that he was given a desk job at first, when he had recovered, but it was no substitute for his old job. He was only fifty-seven at this point, and I would guess he chafed at the lack of activity, but I think he was overly bitter that his life had changed. Don't misunderstand me, though, he struck me as a nice guy, but I think there are some subjects that really set him off and would make him difficult to work with.

'Anyway, he was finally shunted off into early retirement a year later, with a decent pension but no purpose in life. Sits in his cottage a lot of the time. As walking's tricky, he watches the world go by

— more specifically, the boats. Because the medication messes up his sleep pattern, he finds it hard to sleep soundly, so he's taken to watching the sea at night as well as during the day.

'Old George starts to notice some odd things. A couple of times a month, he sees a boat coming across from the direction of the French mainland in the dead hours of the night. Now, it's not unheard of for people to like night sailing, but it is unusual, so it caught his attention. There was also the fact that it wasn't just one boat making the crossing each time. There were four or five that seemed to be taking the same course on different nights.'

'So, some people like travelling at night, and maybe the course they follow is just the best one for those waters,' Shaw commented, playing devil's advocate.

'Just what I was thinking.' Ryland nodded. 'Until George said that this started soon after his old pals had been part of a push by the police to close down a smuggling operation on the other side of Jersey. It had been a success, and landed a big fish from France that they'd had their eyes on for years. George had been told about it by a couple of his colleagues, and rejoiced with them; but then, about two months later, he started to notice these boats.

'He mentioned them to his friends, and at first they were very interested, but when they liaised with the police there seemed to be no illicit substances or goods coming into the island. They would keep an eye out for any signs of it starting up again, but there was no law against sailing at night.'

'Can the police or coastguards do 'stop and search' with boats?' Shaw asked curiously.

'The police certainly can, but not without good reason.'

'So, I'm assuming the story doesn't just end there.' Shaw said. 'What happened next?'

Ryland did not answer immediately. He was looking out for a side turning. 'There it is,' he muttered, and swung onto a rather narrower road.

'George, having nothing much better

to do, got himself a really good pair of binoculars and started making notes on the vessels that he saw from his window. If his notes are accurate he's up half the night, most nights; and bear in mind that he's been doing this for nearly a year now! Anyway, a pattern started to emerge. Between one and three times a month, a motorboat, one out of a pool of six, comes over from France and heads off through St Catherine's Bay and further north. It's usually between two and four in the morning.' He pulled into a passing point and turned to Shaw.

'Can you give me the map in your glove compartment? I want to check something.'

After a quick look, he nodded. 'It must be along here.'

'Do you want to tell me where we're going?' Shaw asked curiously, but not minding if Ryland wanted to keep it a secret for some big reveal moment.

'I will. At the appropriate point in the story,' Ryland replied, following the road as it meandered through the Jersey countryside. 'George Bisson was increasingly fascinated by the movements of these mysterious boats and, once he felt he had established the pattern, he drove to the next headland along from his bay — a spit of land at St Catherine's with a long breakwater. He set up for the night with his binoculars and a flask of tea, and waited to catch sight of one of the six boats, or any others that were around at that time.

'Around three o'clock in the morning, he finally saw the lights of a boat rounding the breakwater and continuing north. It was too far away at that point for him to be sure, but it certainly looked like one of the vessels. George followed the boat with his binoculars until it went out of sight, then started his car and drove north along the coast, much as we just did.

'He had an idea that it might have been turning when he last saw it; and sure enough, when he got to a little bay, he saw the boat had stopped a short way out to shore.'

Shaw tore his eyes away from the

picturesque cottages he had been admiring and started to pay more attention. 'So we're headed to that bay?' he asked.

'Eventually, yes, but there's somewhere else I want to see first. Nearly there now.'

The road had been climbing gently uphill, and now they came up out onto a plateau and could see the sea once more. Ryland pulled the car over onto the grass and opened his door.

The two of them walked to the edge of the lip of the hill and looked down.

'Down there is Fliquet Bay where the boat weighed anchor.' Ryland gestured to a house perched on the hill about halfway between them and the sea. It was a pretty, white, Victorian-style building with a large garden.

Looking down at the house, Shaw noted the police cars parked in the driveway. 'I take it this is where Harry Scadden met his maker?'

'Exactly,' Ryland answered. He sounded both satisfied and excited, and there was a nervous energy coming off him that was almost palpable. 'I knew I wouldn't be able to get close to the house by just going down his drive. The police are keeping people out, but George said you can see it really well from here.'

There was a fresh breeze on the hill, taking the edge off the hot sun overhead; and it would have been one of the most beautiful places Shaw had ever seen, with the lush green grass punctuated by wild flowers and the backdrop of the bay below, were it not for the ugly and sinister addition of the blue-and-white tape cordoning off the entrance to an old barn at the end of the garden below them.

* * *

The sea really was hypnotic, Shaw decided. He had been watching the gently undulating water, sparkling in the afternoon sun, while he waited for Ryland. The reporter had wanted to get some photographs of Scadden's house from their vantage point. Shaw left him to it.

There was nothing illegal about photographing the dead man's home, but he had no wish to be an active participant. He wondered what Louisa's reaction would be if she were there, and thought that it would probably be a mixture of disapproval and a resigned acceptance that reporters have a job to do as well.

He knew that there had been times when the media coverage of a crime had led to important information being brought to the police's attention, and he hoped that his friend's activities might be beneficial in the long run, but it still creeped him out.

Staring out to sea, he tried to focus on the waves, and not on the picture his imagination was conjuring up: a body turning slightly as it hung from a beam.

'Right. I've got what I need. We can go,' Ryland said, his head appearing as he clambered back up the slope.

Shaw shook himself properly awake and took one last look at the view before joining Ryland in the car. 'Did you get to see much?' he asked.

'Not a lot, as you'd expect, but I got a decent shot of the house and the barn. There may well be a picture of Scadden himself on his company's website, and if not, I'm sure I'll be able to find one somewhere. Do you want a lift back to St Helier or somewhere else? I'm going to be kicking my heels until tonight.'

'What's happening tonight?'

'Sorry, I thought I'd said. George Bisson invited me to come back later to meet an acquaintance of his. Not a friend, he was careful to point out. Supposedly it's someone who can get me some real inside information. George doesn't like the guy, but says that he's a necessary evil.'

'Are you sure you know what you're getting into, Ben? It's starting to sound dodgy to me,' Shaw said worriedly. 'If Scadden *was* killed for his involvement in illegal activities, there are some dangerous people around, people who wouldn't take kindly to a reporter poking his nose in.'

'Honestly, Nick! It isn't like working in a war zone. I'm not going to do anything stupid, just get enough credible information to take away and work up into a piece of investigative journalism. I found out a lot in Devonshire, but if I can get something really juicy here it'll give the article some real weight. Maybe even take it into the big league.' Ryland spoke earnestly. 'I need to deliver the goods on this if I'm going to get past the hack work and start making a name for myself.'

'Okay!' Shaw said, raising his hands in defeat. 'Just asking.'

'It'll be fine. You'll see. Now, where do you want to go?'

Shaw reached into the glove compartment and pulled out the map. There were several possibilities. He could go back to St Helier and take another bus out to the western side of the island, as he had planned, or take a look at the north coast as they were already nearly there.

His eyes wandering over the map, he found himself drawn back to the Jersey War Tunnels. He had planned to do that attraction with Ryland anyway, as the reporter had always been interested in the Second World War — so why not now? He looked at the clock on the dashboard — it was twelve minutes past two, so they would have time.

'If you've got a free afternoon, we could go and do the War Tunnels?' he suggested, pointing to the position on the map. 'It's probably about half an hour, if we don't get lost.'

'I'm up for that,' Ryland said, a broad smile on his face. They headed away from the coast and Scadden's beautiful house with its forlorn, blue-and-white reminder of violent death.

Further up the hill, hidden in a copse of trees, Harland lowered his binoculars. So that was George Bisson's eager little newshound, he thought to himself. He should be easy enough to nudge in the right direction. Bisson had not said anything about Ryland having an accomplice with him, though.

Harland's eyes looked speculatively at the departing car. He would have to find out a little more about the two of them. With Scadden no longer around, his best source of blackmail had dried up, and he could not risk having a couple of reporters unearthing the wrong stories. He stowed the binoculars in his jacket, and took the partially hidden path from Scadden's property down to Fliquet Bay where he had left his car. He had a lot to set in motion before his official meeting with Ryland that evening.

3

When Shaw finally emerged from the War Tunnels, he felt poised somewhere between disturbed and heartened. The retelling of the islanders' life during the German occupation of the Channel Islands was accomplished and detailed, but what really had the most impact was the physicality of the tunnels themselves.

The stark, seemingly endless corridors, planned as an underground hospital by the German forces, were chilling; and the exhibits illustrated the moral difficulties as well as the practical ones of life during the war.

'I'm sure I never got taught any of that at school,' Ryland observed. He was leafing through a book in the visitors' shop.

'Me neither. I would have sworn blind that the Germans never conquered any of the British Isles.'

Ryland nodded. 'Makes you wonder

what you would have done if you'd been living here at the time. Fraternise, sabotage, or somewhere in the middle?'

'Not a choice I'd like to be faced with,' Shaw said with some conviction.

'Oh, I don't know. It must have had exciting moments,' Ryland mused. 'Strange though. To be both part of and somehow separate from the main sweep of the war.'

'I don't know if you can call it separate!' Shaw protested. 'Surely the people on the islands were far more involved than most of mainland Britain?'

'I don't mean it like that. It's more that, after they were invaded, it was like the other shoe had dropped — the worst had already happened. I don't think there was any fighting as such here. Maybe it was more like being forgotten. Churchill certainly abandoned them, didn't he?'

'Yes, but didn't you read the bits saying that a fair number of residents were sent to prisoner-of-war camps in Germany, and some people died there before liberation?'

They continued their discussion as they

drove back to St Helier and pulled into the hotel. Switching topics, they stopped for a coffee in the lounge, and spread a map of Jersey out on the coffee table.

'So, where are we going to stay tomorrow night?' Ryland asked.

'I don't know yet,' Shaw replied somewhat absently.

'I thought you had it all worked out! This is your stock-in-trade, isn't it?' Ryland exclaimed.

'It's not a problem. I want to see how hard it is to find accommodation at short notice. I'll do a phone-round tonight and let you know over breakfast.'

Ryland looked sceptically at Shaw.

'It'll be fine, I've done it before and I've never drawn a blank.'

'Well, okay. I'm due to see George Bisson and this other guy in a couple of hours, and I want to get my notes in order. They might have some good stuff for me about Scadden.' Ryland drained his cup and got up to leave.

'I hope it goes well tonight, Ben,' Shaw said.

'So do I. See you in the morning.'

Ryland turned and walked to the stairs.

Shaw stayed in the lounge, using his phone to search for possible accommodation, and marking the locations on the map with sachets of sugar from the pot that had come with their coffee. He was quite absorbed in the task, and when he realised that someone was standing over him, he looked up in surprise.

The stranger looked roughly the same age as him, late thirties or early forties, and was wearing a T-shirt with a map of Jersey on it. He had on sunglasses and a baseball cap, and a large, expensive camera was slung around his neck.

Shaw had already decided the man was an American tourist, and was slightly surprised when the stranger started talking with a clearly German accent.

'Excuse me. Could I ask for your help?' the stranger said, removing his sunglasses to reveal more of his tanned face and a pair of grey eyes. 'I'm trying to find somewhere called Waney, but it does not seem to exist on my map. You seem to know what you're doing.'

'Oh, well, I'm new to the island but I'll

try. Here, join me.' Shaw gestured to the chair that Ryland had recently vacated.

The man sat down and put a small rucksack on the floor beside the table. 'I would have asked at the desk, but the man there is very busy.'

Shaw looked over at the Reception desk and saw that there was a large group of people, seemingly checking in.

'So, you're looking for somewhere called *Waney*?'

'Yes, but I don't know how it is spelled. Many of the names here are confusing.'

'That's true. Do you know anything about it? Is it coastal or inland?'

'It is a beach, but apart from that, nothing.'

'Well, that narrows it down a bit,' Shaw replied cheerfully. He had always loved maps and did not mind deciphering names. He ran his finger round the coastline for a few minutes, but had arrived back at St Helier none the wiser. Then he turned the sound *Waney* over in his head, bearing in mind the strong French influence on place names in Jersey. A moment later, he moved his finger thoughtfully back to the south-west coast.

'I've a feeling I've seen something round here, but I'm not sure,' he murmured, trying to catch an elusive memory. Then his slight frown cleared. 'I think I might know where it is.'

He flipped open his guidebook and ran his finger down the index until he came to the Os. 'Here we are!' he said triumphantly and held out the book to the German stranger. 'Do you see this name?'

The man looked at it perplexedly and raised his eyebrows.

Shaw laughed and said: 'It's all in the pronunciation. This is Ouaisne Bay, commonly called *Waynay* Bay by the locals. I'll bet this is the one you want.'

The stranger stared at the entry for a moment and then smiled delightedly. 'It must be the one. Thank you. Let me buy you a drink.'

Shaw glanced at his watch. It was a little after six. 'Okay, I'll have a pint of beer if you're sure.'

The man returned from the bar with

two beers and set them on the table. 'I'm Kristian Beck,' he said, holding out his hand.

'Nick Shaw,' replied Shaw, shaking hands with Beck. 'So, why are you so keen to find Ouaisne Bay?'

Beck smiled. 'It's because of my grandfather. He used to talk about the beach a lot when I was a boy.'

'Did he come here on holiday then?' Shaw asked.

'No, he came here in quite a different way. He was posted to Jersey during the war,' Beck replied.

'Oh!' Shaw felt a little unsure of how to react. Having just been educated about that time, he knew that there were still a lot of raw nerves in Jersey about the occupying Germans.

'He was only here for a few months in 1941, but he always said it was the only good time for him until the war ended. Here, I have a picture of him from then.'

Beck rummaged in his rucksack and drew out a notebook. Inside was a photograph showing a smiling young man sitting on a sandy beach in bright sunshine.

'His crossing to Jersey was the first time he ever saw the sea, and he fell in love with it.'

'Did he say much about what it was like being on the island as an occupying force?' Shaw asked curiously.

'Not really. He wasn't a good soldier, though. Spent most of the time dreaming about home, except for when he was here. He learned to sail in Jersey, and later on he taught my mother and then me. He always meant to come back here, but he never made it, so this summer I finally got over here to see for myself. My plane landed this afternoon, and I thought I would have a nice meal and find my grandfather's beach on the map. That was when I ran into the problem of the name.'

'Well I hope you have a good holiday here. Ouaisne Bay is beautiful, I was there with a friend last night, at a pub called The Smuggler's Inn. You should try it.'

Shaw felt himself relaxing after the busy day. The beer was doing its job, and when the first one was finished he bought another round for them.

An hour later, he remembered that he was supposed to be finding accommodation for Ryland and himself, and reluctantly said goodbye to Beck, who was going to be staying at the *Pomme d'Or* for a few days.

After a bit of ringing round, Shaw found a guesthouse on the north coast which had two rooms available. More tired than he expected to be, he gave up on the idea of going out for supper. Instead, he contented himself with a packet of crisps left over from lunch and all of the biscuits on the tea and coffee tray, before falling asleep in front of the television.

★　★　★

'Oh, come on!' Shaw muttered under his breath. He had first texted Ryland an hour ago to see if he was ready for breakfast, but received no reply. The lack of a meal the previous night had left him ravenous, and he was eager to get downstairs and eat something hearty. The second and third texts had also gone unanswered, so he was phoning the mobile in the hope that the persistent ringtone might wake Ryland up, or get him out of the bath if that was the hold-up.

The phone switched to the answering service, and Shaw hung up. He decided to have breakfast himself and let Ryland catch up with him, but there was still no sign of him by the time he had finished eating. He returned upstairs and knocked on Ryland's door.

'Wake up, Ben!' he called, but there was no reply. He carried on knocking, becoming worried. A thought occurred to him, and he took out his phone and called Ryland's number.

He could hear it ringing through his handset, but could not hear a corresponding ring through the door, not even with his ear pressed up against it. Ryland's phone had a distinctive ring, the *Ride of the Valkyries* at full blast. He should have been able to hear it if the phone had been in the room.

Shaw stepped away from the door.

What if Ryland had never come back last night?

He walked down to Reception, thinking hard. First things first. He had to make sure Ryland was not in the room, perhaps ill. He might have lost his phone somewhere. Hotel staff were generally wary of invading a guest's privacy at the behest of another guest — although this seldom stopped them waltzing in for housekeeping duties with a perfunctory knock before unlocking the door. He hoped that the receptionist would be reasonable about it.

'Good morning, sir. How can I help you?' The desk clerk smiled cheerily.

'I'm extremely concerned about my friend, Mr Ryland. He was supposed to meet me for breakfast and I can't get any response from his room or from his mobile. Can you please check on him?'

The clerk looked worried and said, 'I'll need to ask my manager. Just one moment.' He left for a back room and returned with a much older man.

'Can you please get the door of the room open and check on him?' Shaw asked. He was getting more worried that something had happened. It was very unlike Ryland to miss a scheduled meeting without letting him know.

'Do you have any reason to believe that your friend is ill?' the manager asked.

Shaw decided to bend the truth a little. 'Well, I'm sure he mentioned something about insulin one time, but he doesn't really like to talk about his health.'

'You think he may be in a state of collapse?' The manager looked worried too now. Having an ambulance turn up at the hotel was never a welcome event. 'Okay, I'll go and see if Mr Ryland is in need of any help.'

Shaw accompanied the hotel manager back to Ryland's room, and after there was still no reply to their knocking, the door was unlocked.

The bed cover was slightly rumpled, but it had obviously not been slept in. Shaw came in before the manager could stop him, and strode quickly into the bathroom. There was no sign of Ryland, although his razor and toothbrush were still by the sink.

'He's not here!' Shaw exclaimed.

'Perhaps your friend got up early and went for a walk? He may have forgotten that you were supposed to meet up,' the manager suggested. He seemed far less concerned now that they had not found an ill or dead guest.

'Look at the bed. I really don't think he slept here last night,' Shaw protested. He was getting angrier by the minute, and more worried.

'Well, we don't insist that our guests stay in residence for all of their stay. He was quite at liberty to sleep somewhere else. I think we should leave, sir.'

The manager opened the bedroom door and waited pointedly for Shaw to go.

A quick scan of the room showed that the bag Ryland had been carrying yesterday, the one that held his camera, recorder and notebook, was missing. Shaw reluctantly left and went back downstairs with the manager.

'Would you know if Ben came back in last night?'

'Only if there was a particular reason to notice him. Guests tend to take their room keys with them these days, so we can't keep tabs on them. There would have been someone on Reception until midnight, and there's always a member of staff available through the night if necessary. If your friend had needed assistance, then Alex would remember.'

'Can you ask him?'

'Well, he may be catching up on sleep. He's not due to start work until midday.'

The manager looked searchingly at Shaw. 'Don't you think it's likely that Mr Ryland has just made other arrangements and forgotten to let you know?'

It was possible, Shaw had to admit to himself. If Ryland had been hot on the trail of something exciting, then he could have stayed out all night, perhaps with George Bisson. Maybe he was overreacting.

He took his leave of the manager and wandered through to the lounge, thinking hard. Ryland had mentioned that he was expected at the coastguard's house at eight o'clock, to meet up with this mysterious acquaintance of Bisson's. He had certainly expected to be back for breakfast at the very least, and it was not like him to just leave Shaw hanging.

It was surely too early to be panicking, though. Ryland might just have been caught up somewhere. Might have lost his phone. He did not want to report his friend as missing, only to have him saunter in half an hour later.

Shaw's eyes had been flicking round the room as he thought and now they alighted on the selection of newspapers on a side table. The top one was the *Jersey Evening Post* and he could just make out the front page. The headline story was about proposed changes to laws that would affect the island's reputation as a tax haven, but lower down there was a photograph with the accompanying line: *Official confirmation: businessman Harry Scadden murdered.*

That made Shaw's mind up for him. He would have to go to the police.

* * *

'Right. So I think I have all the details, sir. Your friend, Mr Ryland, was expected to

60

meet you for breakfast this morning and didn't arrive. He was not in his room, and his bed appeared not to have been slept in. You tried to call him on his mobile but he didn't answer, and you believe that the bag he had for everyday use was not in the hotel room. When you looked in the car park, the hired car he was driving had gone.' The police officer looked enquiringly at Shaw for confirmation.

'Yes, that's all correct,' Shaw answered. He had thought to look for the car as he left the hotel for the police station.

'And you're particularly concerned because of two factors. Firstly, that you're both due to check out from the *Pomme d'Or* today, and he did not yet know where you would be going on to. Secondly, that Mr Ryland was currently investigating a story which he thought was linked to the recent murder of Harry Scadden and to suspicions of a smuggling ring operating in the islands. The last time you saw him, he was planning to visit a Mr George Bisson and an unnamed associate of his in relation to this.' The officer finished and surveyed the information.

'I may be overreacting. I hope I am, but if Ben's had an accident or if he's . . . Oh, I don't know!' Shaw felt he was floundering to explain. 'If he's somehow got into trouble over this smuggling thing, he'll need help. I didn't want to just wait and hope he'd turn up.'

The officer regarded him with some sympathy. 'You've done the right thing, sir. People can feel awkward when they report an adult as missing. Particularly when it's not a family member. If Mr Ryland turns up wondering what all the fuss is about, then there's no harm done. If, on the other hand, there is a need for our involvement, then it helps that you've reported it immediately.'

He rose from his chair. 'Would you mind waiting a few minutes while I speak with the team handling Mr Scadden's death?'

'Not at all,' Shaw answered, and watched as the officer left the room. He leant back in his chair with some relief. He had been worried that the police would be dismissive of his tale. In films, the police often seemed to be reluctant to take missing persons seriously, at least in the first instance.

The more he thought about it, the more strange it seemed. Ryland was one of the most fanatically 'connected' people he knew. He always had his phone charged up and turned on. True, if the phone had got broken he would be stuck, but surely he would have found a way to get a message through.

After a longer wait than he had expected, the door opened again and a different officer came in.

He was probably a little younger than Shaw, and rather on the thin side, wearing a nondescript grey suit that did not fit him very well. His eyes, however, were lively and intelligent.

'Good morning, Mr Shaw. Thank you for coming to see us.' The policeman shook hands and sat down. 'I'm Detective Chief Inspector Keith Raven. I'm working on the Scadden investigation, and I interviewed Mr Ryan yesterday. I'm very sorry to hear that he may be missing.'

'I could be wrong, but it isn't like Ben.'

'We'll certainly look into it. One of my colleagues has checked with the hospital, and no one has been admitted who fits your description.'

'That was quick!' Shaw said with surprise.

'There's only one General Hospital on Jersey, so it doesn't take long. I understand that you don't have any contact details for George Bisson?'

'No, although I can tell you roughly where he lives.' Shaw drew his map out of his bag and found the St Catherine's area on the east coast. 'From what Ben said, Bisson must live somewhere along this section.'

'Good, we should be able to find him from this. I'll get someone on to it right away. The first thing we can do is ask Mr Bisson if your friend reached him; and, if so, when he left. I would also like to contact Mr Ryland's family to ask if he has been in contact with them since he left you yesterday evening.'

Shaw felt a wave of guilt. It had not even occurred to him to think about a family.

'I'm afraid I know next to nothing about Ben's situation. I mean, he isn't married, and I don't think there's a girlfriend around at the moment, but I've no idea about parents or siblings.'

'That's okay. You gave us the newspaper he works for. They should have next-of-kin details,' Raven said. 'Where will you be staying for the next few days? Will you be checking out of the *Pomme d'Or* later today?'

'Oh, God. I hadn't really thought yet,' Shaw groaned. Being at the police station was bringing home the possibility that Ryland really was in trouble. 'Maybe I should see if I can stay on there. Ben doesn't know where I've booked us in next.'

'That may be for the best, if they have room. I need to go over to the hotel myself and have a word with the manager. Would you like a lift?'

'Er, yes please.' Shaw was a little surprised, but it would be handy to get back and see if he could extend the booking. It was also possible that Ryland would be there already.

'Right.' Raven stood up. 'I have a few things to tie up here, so would you mind waiting at the front desk?'

Shaw readily agreed, and it was not long before they were driving the short distance to the *Pomme d'Or*.

'If it isn't possible to stay on at the hotel, I'll get them to find you an alternative nearby. I expect that this will be resolved quickly and that your friend is just delayed somewhere,' Raven said.

'I hope so too, but I really don't like the fact that the story he was investigating includes a murder. What if Ben really was on to something?'

'That is why I want to act quickly. We'll keep you informed, as well as Mr Ryland's family, when we get their details. It's a shame you don't have a photograph of him, but we should be able to get hold of one fairly easily. While you were waiting, we found an address for George Bisson, who might be able to clear this all up.' Raven pulled into the hotel car park.

Once inside, Raven talked to the manager, whose face fell at the thought of an official enquiry. Both rooms were

66

available for at least one more night, and Raven asked that Ryland's not be disturbed until the police had been able to check it over.

Having impressed on the staff that any message relating to Ryland must be immediately communicated to the police — including, of course, his reappearance if that happened — Raven took his leave, saying to Shaw: 'If anything occurs to you, any snippet of conversation for example, call the station.'

Feeling restless and uncertain, Shaw went up to his room. He called to cancel the bed and breakfast booking, then sat in a chair looking out of the window. He did not want to do much until he heard from the police.

Perhaps Ryland was still with Bisson. They might have gone off last night to stake out that bay. That would account for him not sleeping at the hotel — but why had he not called in the morning? Okay, his phone could have got lost, broken, or even stolen, but he could have called from Bisson's house on their return; or from a public telephone, or from any number of pubs or hotels on the island.

Shaw made himself a coffee while he thought about this. It was this continued silence that was worrying him. It did not fit with Ryland's character at all. He was the kind of person who answered his mobile in the cinema and annoyed everyone; who would suddenly break off from a conversation to make a call because he had just had a great idea. If Ryland was out of contact, it was because something was wrong.

Shaw looked at his watch. It was nearly eleven o'clock. Reflecting that there was never a good time to phone Louisa at work, he decided to call her on the off-chance that she would be able to talk, albeit briefly.

To his relief, she answered and sounded cheerful.

'Hi Nick! How's the holiday going?'

'There's a problem. Ben's gone missing.'

'*What!* Tell me what happened,' Louisa demanded, her voice instantly serious.

Shaw quickly related the events and

waited for her response. There was a pause, and then she asked: 'How seriously do you think the police are taking it?'

'More so than I had expected, actually. I thought I'd have to convince them to take it up, but the Detective Inspector is already on it.'

'That's what I find worrying,' Louisa said. 'The man who was hanged — did that happen before you got to Jersey?'

'Yes, his body was found the day we arrived.'

'But do you know when he died?'

'Not specifically, but does it matter?'

'It might. Think about it. A man thought by the police to be connected with smuggling dies the day that a reporter investigating smuggling arrives. It would make me look for a connection if it was my case.'

'God! Do you think our coming here caused someone to kill Scadden?'

'Well, it's a hell of a coincidence, wouldn't you say? Look, I don't want to be alarmist, but I agree with you that this really isn't like Ben.'

'Why did you say you found it worrying

that Raven's taking it so seriously?'

'There are two possibilities that I can think of. Either they know a lot more than they've released about Scadden, and know that anyone sniffing around would be in real danger; or they think that Ben was involved with Scadden's murder himself.'

'You must be kidding!' Shaw exclaimed.

'I'm sorry, Nick. I'm just telling it how it is. Depending on when Scadden died, they could theorise that Ben had gone to interview his suspected smuggler on the day you both arrived. That could have set off a heated argument that ended up in a death, whether accidental or otherwise.'

'But there would have been no time!' Shaw protested. 'We didn't get in until after four. Then we were in the hotel bar for a while, in plain view, and after that we went for dinner. It was at least ten o'clock when we called it a night.'

'And considering the newspaper was carrying the news of the discovery the next morning, the death must have occurred reasonably early the day before.' Louisa considered the facts for a moment. 'I think that Ben, and you for that matter, must be in the clear.'

'I should hope so! Is there anything I should be doing, or do I just let the police get on with it?'

'I don't think there's anything you *can* do. You've already done the right thing by reporting Ben as missing. The police will tell the family, if there is one. All you can do is sit tight for now. Be available if you're needed, and if you haven't heard any more by about six o'clock, you could call the station and ask if there have been any developments. Nick, I'm so sorry I can't be there with you. There's no way I can leave work at the moment.'

'I know. Don't worry about me. For all I know, Ben's off on a boat somewhere, having sent a message that hasn't got through.' Shaw tried to sound positive.

'I'll call you tonight. Take care, Nick.'

'Speak to you later,' Shaw said, and rang off. He decided to go downstairs and sit in the lounge. If Ryland returned, he would see him, but he was beginning to worry that that was increasingly unlikely.

4

By five o'clock, Shaw had read all the papers, skimmed through the tourist literature at Reception, and talked with every member of staff he saw. He was keen to know if anyone had seen Ryland leave the *Pomme d'Or* the previous evening.

Frustratingly, none of them had any information for him, although the sympathetic receptionist brought him over a plate of sandwiches 'on the house'. He was restless, tired and stressed, and when Raven walked into the lobby he leapt to his feet.

'Any news?' Shaw asked, crossing to the desk where Raven was standing.

'We know a little more,' Raven answered. He turned to the receptionist and said: 'Is there a quiet room we could use for a short time?'

'The small conference room is free, sir. Through here.' The receptionist led them down a corridor and into a neat room with a table set up for meetings.

Shaw was trying not to second-guess what Raven's news would be, but it was hard not to wonder if the Detective Inspector had asked for a private room to impart bad news.

Raven shut the door and took a seat. 'I've seen George Bisson, and he confirms that Mr Ryland did visit him last night to discuss their theories about smuggling on Jersey. They chatted for a little over an hour, and Mr Ryland left somewhere close to ten o'clock.'

'But, Ben said that there would be another person there — someone who he thought Bisson didn't like.'

'Yes, I was glad you had told us that earlier. It didn't seem to occur to Mr Bisson that he ought to tell us about his other guest until I raised it. Then he admitted that another friend, Dominic Harland, had dropped by briefly. I'll be interviewing Mr Harland later.'

'Did you believe Bisson?' Shaw asked bluntly.

'I've no reason not to at this stage,'

Raven replied cagily. He leant forward with his elbows on the table. 'Mr Bisson seemed genuinely surprised and upset that Mr Ryland has not been seen since last night. He invited me to look over the cottage, which I did, and he suggested that if this was a real disappearance, not just some kind of misunderstanding, then he would definitely suspect some form of foul play. He's of the opinion that there are some dangerous people involved.'

'And are there?'

Raven looked very directly at Shaw. 'There are some aspects of our investigation and some avenues we will be pursuing which I can't discuss. We'll keep you updated about anything that relates to your friend.' He paused before continuing.

'We contacted Mr Ryland's employers, and their records only have one family member listed as next of kin. He has an elderly father in a care home, who is unfortunately in the late stages of dementia, and the home has no knowledge of any other relatives. We may turn up a cousin or similar with a little more research into the records, but at the moment you're the closest thing to a relative we are aware of, and the best source of information about Mr Ryland.'

'God! I'll do anything I can to help, but I've only known Ben for about three years.' Shaw felt somewhat uncomfortable, and realised he had been subconsciously waiting for a parent or sibling to step in. Rather ashamed, he pulled himself together. 'Did you get hold of a photograph of Ben?'

'Yes, the paper sent us several images. We'll distribute those to all our officers; and, if need be, to the local media. I should get back to the station now, but I'll be in touch.'

Raven rose and they walked back down the corridor to the lobby. 'Most people who are reported missing turn up safe and sound, you know, and Jersey is generally a pretty peaceful place.'

It wasn't for Harry Scadden, thought Shaw.

★　★　★

By ten o'clock of the following day, Shaw had taken a bus up to the north-west of Jersey, to L'Etaq. He had no particular aim in mind, but wanted a change from St Helier.

It was fresher this morning and a breeze had picked up. The landscape was more rugged than the south coast, and as he walked along the beach he found his spirits lifting a little with the expanse of sea before him. He absent-mindedly picked up a few stones and pieces of sea glass, rattling them in his pocket.

The afternoon he had spent fretting at the hotel had stiffened up his back, and he took the opportunity now to consciously stretch his muscles. Although no one would have called him sporty, he disliked being inactive.

Whether he was working on an article at home or out researching on foot, he much preferred to be doing something rather than just relaxing. It was one of the reasons his work suited him — there was always something to be getting on with. Now, however, he felt hamstrung by Ryland's disappearance.

He could not carry on with his plans for the week — nor would he have wanted to — but he needed something to do, or he would simply brood.

Much of yesterday afternoon had been occupied with replaying all the conversations he had had with Ryland in Jersey, looking for any kind of clue. He certainly did not think that this absence was planned. It was still possible that an opportunity had come up that was too good to miss.

The stealthy surveillance of a suspect's house was just the kind of chance Ryland would have jumped at, as was the offer of a speedboat ride to France or something similar, but in either case it would have been easy to get a message through to the hotel, if not to Shaw himself.

The only scenarios that made sense were the worst ones — abduction, injury or death. Of the three, the most hopeful one was that he had fallen down a cliff and been hurt, but even that one did not bode well. It was now over thirty-five hours since he had left Bisson's house.

If, of course, he had been alive and well at that point.

Shaw took the stones and sea-smoothed glass nuggets out of his pocket, and weighed them in his hand for a moment. Then he drew back his arm and hurled them out towards the sea. He walked back to the bus stop, checking his phone yet again for any missed messages, but there were none.

He felt the need to keep moving, and when the bus arrived he asked the driver what would be the longest journey he could do.

'From here, that would be over to St Catherine's on the east coast,' the driver answered. He pulled one of the timetables out of its holder. 'You'd have to go back to Liberation Station and catch the 2A. It should take about two hours, so if you want a long bus ride, that's the one for you.'

Shaw paid for the ticket and sat down. Travelling by bus usually distracted him, and he hoped that today would be no exception. The fact that his random choice of destination would set him down near to the last place that Ryland was seen had not been lost on him.

★   ★   ★

The journey helped to take Shaw's mind off his worries, particularly when a couple of garrulous teenage boys got on at St Helier. Listening to their conversations, he was both pleasantly distracted and heartily glad that he was past that stage of his life.

The journey across the island on a sunny, breezy day took him through beautiful, varied landscapes, and he fetched up at St Catherine's confirmed in his appreciation of Jersey. Even with the cloud of Ryland's disappearance hanging over him, he was captivated.

St Catherine's proved to be a coastal area of land with only a few houses, although Shaw had seen there were some more set a little way back from the coast. A long breakwater stretched out into the sea, the same breakwater that Bisson had seen the suspicious boats rounding in the dead hours of the night.

He walked out to the end of it and looked to the right. The bay curved round in a wide arc, and he could make out a good few cottages that might be Bisson's. To the left, he saw what he supposed must be Fliquet Bay, and somewhere on the hill above it would be Harry Scadden's house.

He checked his watch and saw that it was close to one o'clock. He had not felt like breakfast at the hotel, and was hungry now. There had been a café at the beginning of the breakwater, so he walked back and ordered a sandwich and a drink.

His food had only just arrived when his mobile rang. 'Hello?' Shaw said.

'Hello, Mr Shaw. It's Detective Chief Inspector Raven here.'

'Have you found anything?'

'Not as such, but I wanted to let you know that we've released a statement to the local newspaper and television stations. There should be a piece in the paper tomorrow morning, with a photograph of Mr Ryland that might jog people's memories.'

'Okay. Hopefully that will do something. Did you get to speak with Harland?' Shaw asked.

'Not yet, but we will,' said Raven. 'He's been out all day.'

'I take it you'd like me to stay on at the *Pomme d'Or* another night?'

'It would make things easier if you at least stay in St Helier. I know you're booked to sail back on Monday. If you'd prefer to stay somewhere else, that would be fine, but I would like to know where.'

'What if we get to Monday and there's still no sign of Ben? Will I have to stay in Jersey?' Shaw asked. He had been thinking about this on the bus.

'I have absolutely no reason to keep you here, and if you need to return to work or family we'd simply need to make sure we have your home address and telephone number for our records. So far, we haven't tracked down any family members for Mr Ryland other than his father, but you're under no legal obligation to stay. I sincerely hope, though, that we will have found him before Monday.'

'Me too.' There was a pause when

neither spoke, then Shaw broke the silence. 'Do you have any idea what's happened to Ben? Even just a hunch?'

'At the moment I'd rather stick to what factual evidence we have. I'm hopeful that Dominic Harland might shed some light on the situation. Certainly we haven't found the hired car. No one has been brought into any hospital or GP practice who fits Mr Ryland's description; and, fortunately, no body has been found. I know that it's frustrating and very worrying waiting for information, but I can assure you that I will tell you about any developments.'

'And how about the Scadden murder? Have there been any leads there?'

'Possibly, but nothing I can comment on.'

Shaw could see that he had got all he could from Raven for now. 'Okay, well, keep in touch. I'll certainly stay at the hotel tonight.'

'I will, sir.'

Shaw put his mobile away and considered his options. He was sorely tempted to see if he could get somewhere by himself. Louisa had said he should leave it to the police, but Scadden's murder could well be taking up most of their resources. He felt like he was letting his friend down by not doing anything. At the very least, he could be out looking for him.

Making up his mind, he checked the bus timetable. He was going to go back to St. Helier, get a car, and start searching.

⋆   ⋆   ⋆

It felt good to be driving again. Just being behind a wheel gave Shaw a sense of empowerment. He was not a car-lover generally, but being reliant on public transport was beginning to get on his nerves. It also emboldened him, and before he could stop to talk himself out of it, he had pulled over on the outskirts of St Helier to look up Bisson, G. in the phone book.

It had taken some time to hire the car as the company were pressing him to wait until the following morning, but Shaw had a way of being politely immovable when he needed to, and they had eventually caved in and produced a vehicle within a couple of hours.

It was getting on for five o'clock when he found Gull Cottage after parking a short way off and walking back. He knew that he could get into trouble with Raven for approaching Bisson, but he was tired of hanging around, waiting for scraps of information.

There was no doorbell so he knocked on the door. A voice called out from inside: 'I'll be with you in a minute!'

The door was eventually opened by a stocky man with white, receding hair, glasses and a walking stick. 'Yes?' he asked, looking at Shaw with some confusion.

'Hello, Mr Bisson. I'm Nick Shaw, and I hope you'll forgive me for turning up unannounced, but I'm very anxious to find my friend, Ben Ryland.'

'You're a friend of Ben's?' Bisson asked uncertainly. 'Can you prove it?'

Shaw was taken aback. He had not expected this. 'Er, I don't have any kind of document that would do it, but . . . I can tell you that Ben has a real problem with staying still. You probably noticed that he fidgets all the time, doodles on his notebooks, and gets up to fiddle with ornaments. He has what you could call a boyish enthusiasm for excitement, and he's clever and funny. I know that he first contacted you through a researcher called Rick.'

'All right, I believe you. You'd better come in.' Bisson shuffled back to allow Shaw into the small hallway.

'I don't think there's anything I can do to help,' Bisson said, leading Shaw into a comfortable sitting room. 'Are you a reporter too?'

'No, I'm a travel writer,' Shaw replied, taking a seat on the sofa.

'Oh. Ben didn't mention that he was travelling with someone. Sorry to quiz you, but in the circumstances, I've got a bit jumpy.' Bisson took what was clearly his usual place in a large and faded armchair. 'Has there been no news of Ben, then?'

'Nothing at all. The police assure me that they are doing everything they can, but I realised today that I was not.'

'So you're not here in any kind of official capacity?' Bisson pressed.

'None at all. I just want to find Ben, and this seems to be the last place he was seen.'

Bisson sighed. 'I'm so sorry that he's missing. Do you know what he was investigating?'

'Yes, he told me a bit about his research in Devon, and how it had led him here.'

'Well, he was right. There was a real bastard on Jersey, controlling drug trafficking in the waters between here and France in the first instance, and I'm pretty sure that he had a hand in things further afield, although I've no way of proving that.

'When I heard from Rick a few days ago, it seemed like the answer to a prayer. I'd tried to get the local reporters interested in my story, but they were too scared to tackle the subject unless there were actual arrests. I couldn't push the police when they all said that there was not enough evidence.'

'Are we talking about Harry Scadden

here?' Shaw interrupted.

'Of course we are! He was the ringleader, right up until Monday when something finally went wrong for him.' Bisson thumped the arm of his chair. 'I was so close to nailing him. So close! I knew that he was keeping the shipments somewhere on his property, and I'd just managed to find out where. We could have got the police out there and caught him red-handed.'

'I take it that by 'we' you don't mean you and Ben? He didn't come into this until after Scadden was found dead.'

'No. I got to know a man called Dominic Harland. He has also been keeping tabs on Scadden, and suggested that we join forces.'

Bisson leaned down and rapped the side of his leg, making a dull knocking sound. 'My leg got crushed during a rescue, and the surgery I had never sorted it out, so it had to go. I manage all right, but I needed someone able-bodied to help, and Harland was very plausible at first.'

'Harland met Ben, didn't he?' Shaw

asked, remembering that the police had not been able to talk with him yet.

'Yes, he was here on Wednesday night.' Bisson rubbed his hand nervously across his mouth. He was obviously struggling to come to a decision. Finally, he gave an almost imperceptible nod, and took a deep breath.

'I'd better be frank with you. Harland is not someone I would normally associate with. He doesn't care about the immorality of smuggling, or about the blighted lives of drug addicts. His only motivation is lining his own pockets.

'I don't know how he got on to what I was doing, but I suppose I don't exactly keep my mouth shut. Harland offered to help me get evidence against Scadden, but the deal was supposed to be that he would blackmail him for a few months first, and then hand all he knew to the police after he had made enough money.' Bisson looked very tired and there was a bitter twist to his mouth.

'Christ! Did Ben know about this?' Shaw exclaimed, trying to see where this fitted into Ryland's disappearance.

'No, Harland merely said he was a 'concerned citizen', the smarmy bastard. The last thing he wanted was for an exposé to come out in the papers; but when I talked to him about meeting Ben, just after Rick had called me, he liked the idea of having a reporter lined up for the time when he would hang Scadden out to dry. Of course, it was later that day that the news came out about Scadden's death.

'I thought that it was all over then, but Harland let slip that he knew more about Scadden's organisation than he had told me. He said it wouldn't take long for someone to take over the routes, whether it was one of Scadden's cronies or a rival group. When they did, we would be ready to pounce.

'He told Ben about half of the information we have, but we left it that I would be in touch when we knew more. I swear to you that Ben was fine when he left here — excited, even, about the prospect of a scoop, even a delayed one.'

Shaw sat in stunned silence for a long moment, too many questions vying for attention in his mind. Eventually he spoke. 'Have you told all of this to the police?'

Bisson looked more uncomfortable than ever. 'Not quite all of it at first,' he admitted. 'When Detective Chief Inspector Raven and his assistant came to talk to me, I panicked. I didn't want to mention Harland at all, but they knew someone else had been present already, so I just said that he was someone like me who had noticed strange things.

'To be honest, I don't think they believed me anyway. There was a kind of look when I told them Harland's name. I've been half-expecting to be arrested for being an accomplice to blackmail.'

'You do realise that this information might be vital to finding Ben? If Harland's quite prepared to stoop to blackmail, what else might he do?' Shaw was getting angry.

'But there was absolutely no reason to hurt Ben. Harland was pleased with the idea.' Bisson's temperature was also climbing. 'He was annoyed that Scadden had been killed, but he said that we could go ahead with the original plan once he had identified the new ringleaders. I think he has a pretty good idea of who might have done Scadden in. Ben wasn't a threat. He was an asset, don't you see!' Bisson was almost shouting now with a mixture of fear and defiance.

'I do see, and if Ben would have been an asset to *you*, then he would have been a threat to whoever killed Harry Scadden. You all are!' Shaw shouted back.

Bisson stopped, with his mouth slightly open, staring at Shaw. Then he slumped back in his chair and put his head in his hands. 'You're right. Oh God, you're right. I've been fooling myself.'

Shaw pulled his wallet from his pocket and took out a card. 'This is Raven's number. Do you want to dial it or shall I?'

5

The view from Gull Cottage's small garden was beautiful, and Shaw tried to let it soothe him, but without success. Raven and another policeman had arrived at the cottage very soon after Bisson's call, and had settled down to take his revised statement. There had been the obligatory offer of having a solicitor present, but Bisson had waved it aside, saying: 'It wouldn't change what I have to tell you. Then it's up to you what you decide to do.'

The interview had lasted longer than Shaw had expected, and he had spent all of the time on a plastic chair in the garden that overlooked the sea. Raven had given him a look that promised he would need to talk later, but merely asked him to stay out of the sitting room. Shaw was tempted to call Louisa, but decided to leave it for the moment. So he sat and looked out to sea, wondering if all of this would finally lead them to Ryland.

The call came to go back into the house, and he took a seat once more in the sitting room. Bisson looked pale, whereas Raven was energised.

'This could be the breakthrough we needed, both on the Scadden investigation and to find Mr Ryland. I want to bring Dominic Harland in immediately. He has a lot of questions to answer.' Raven turned to Bisson.

'I'm not sure what action will be taken about your role in this. As it stands you were aware that Harland was intending to extort money from Harry Scadden; and that Harland claimed to know, or at least have a strong suspicion about, the identity of Scadden's murderer. By not disclosing this earlier, you could be charged with obstructing the course of justice. At the moment I'm not inclined to take you into custody, but I would advise you to make contact with a lawyer.'

'I understand,' Bisson said quietly.

'Have you heard of Harland before? In an official capacity, I mean,' Shaw asked.

'He's not unknown to us, but he

appears to be branching out from his usual rackets,' Raven answered. 'We'll be going now. Mr Shaw, can I have a word?'

Shaw nodded and went over to Bisson. He held out his hand. 'Thank you for making a clean breast of it, George.'

Bisson took the offered hand and said: 'I'm just sorry I didn't do it straight away.'

The two policemen and Shaw left the cottage and Raven walked Shaw to his car.

'I'm very glad that you got this information for us, but I would ask you not to do any further . . . investigating on your own. Mr Bisson is harmless, but I doubt if everyone involved in this is. Be smart and stay out of trouble.'

Shaw considered this. 'Good advice,' he said after a moment.

Raven seemed to be expecting more for after a pause he asked: 'And will you take it?'

'Would you have got to the bottom of Bisson and Harland's scheme if I hadn't interfered?'

'I'm sure it would have come to light

one way or another, though of course I'm very grateful to — '

Shaw interrupted him. 'Well, Ben might not have time to let things 'come to light'. I'm not going to do anything stupid, but I can't promise more than that.'

So saying, he opened his car door and drove off, the lean figure of Raven slowly decreasing in his rear-view mirror.

★   ★   ★

'*You did what?*' Louisa's voice was incredulous and angry.

'I went to see a disabled pensioner,' Shaw answered calmly. 'He wasn't exactly a threat.'

'How were you to know that he didn't have a gun? That he wouldn't poison your drink? That he didn't have an accomplice there?' Louisa demanded.

'Okay, I didn't know that, but it seemed unlikely; and to be honest, I'm fed up with just sitting and worrying. There's no one else over here who knows Ben, and no one back home except for a senile father and the rest of Ben's friends. I've got a duty to do what I can, Louisa.'

There was a long pause and Shaw could imagine Louisa taking a long breath and forcing herself to 'ditch the anger', as she called it. According to her, anger encouraged bad decisions in police work.

'Well, I don't think you have to feel responsible, but I can understand that you do,' Louisa said. 'Please leave it to the police now, though. I don't like the sound of Harland at all, and anyone who's involved in smuggling has a lot to lose if they get caught. You've only got a couple more days there, and I don't think Raven will insist on you staying on Jersey. He certainly has no grounds to do so. You could come back now if you want.' She left the idea hanging.

'No. I'd rather stay, at least until Monday. Louisa, can you think of anything more I can do — that you approve of, that is?'

'Sensible question,' she said wryly. 'Okay, have you talked to anyone at the newspaper, or to any of Ben's friends? You know them better than me.'

'Not yet.'

'Why not call the editor, or whoever it is? They'd probably be glad to get some more information than the police will be telling them. You could get in touch with any of Ben's friends that you have numbers for as well. Someone might know of a relative, perhaps someone more distant. It can be hard for the police to find those kind of links.' She sighed. 'Just be careful, Nick. I'd come over if I could.'

'I know you would. Don't worry. Even if I wanted to, there's no way I can think of to get any further. It sounds like Harland's gone into hiding, and I've no way of finding either him or the smugglers. I'll do some ringing round to try and find out about Ben's family. I'm sure I've got numbers for Nancy Fleck and Joe Atkins, at least. They've known him a while, and I can get hold of someone at the paper easily enough. I'd better go now, my battery is getting low. Love you.'

'Love you too, and take care.'

'I always do,' Shaw said and rang off. He had made the call from the car park at

St Catherine's Bay, a short distance from Bisson's house. He could just make out Fliquet Bay from there, and was tempted to go over, but could not think of what he might be looking for.

Louisa was talking sense. He decided to drive back to the hotel and make his phone calls from there. If he was lucky, Raven would track down Harland, and there might even be more information before the end of the day. What that information might be, though, he was becoming increasingly worried about.

★ ★ ★

The evening sun was slanting through the windows of Shaw's room by the time he had finished his phone calls. He had got through to Atkins after a few false starts, and explained what was going on. Atkins was able to confirm that Ryland seldom talked about his family, but he had heard that his mother had died at least ten years ago. He knew a couple of other friends of Ben's who Shaw did not, and said that he would contact them to let them know and

98

ask if anyone could shed more light on the family.

'I'll try Sophie first. She went out with Ben for a while, longer than most of them. It's odd, really. He never talks about domestic things. I'd no idea his father was still alive. If I find anything I'll call you.'

It had been easy getting through to Ryland's boss, who had been sympathetic and worried. She had agreed that he was just the kind to go haring off after a story, but equally certain that he would never have stayed out of touch. The police were keeping her informed, but she was certain that they were not telling her everything. 'I mean, what about his phone? You can't tell me they haven't tried to track its location.'

'What do you mean?' Shaw had asked.

'They have the authority to get the mobile companies to see where it was last used. It's not very accurate, but it might give them a clue. When I asked the detective about it, he side-stepped the question; so either they hadn't thought to do it, which is unlikely, or they know but they're not telling.'

Thinking back on the conversation, Shaw wondered if she had been right. It had not occurred to him that the phone could be traced, but surely the police would have tried it. He would have to ask Raven about it; but right at that moment he needed something to eat and something alcoholic to drink.

He did not feel like eating at the hotel, as the staff there kept asking if there was any news. He understood their concern, but it was wearing. He left his room and walked downstairs, saw that the desk clerk was preoccupied with a telephone call, and slipped out of the hotel.

He had no real idea where to go, so he let himself wander towards the centre of St Helier and stopped when he saw a pub that was not too crowded.

A meal duly arrived at his table and he ate it automatically, his mind turning over all the possibilities of Ryland's continued absence.

'Nick, I found it! The exact place the picture was taken!' An enthusiastic voice roused Shaw from his brooding. Beck was standing by his table, a broad smile on his face.

'Oh, that's great.' Shaw managed to drag his mind back to the present.

Beck sat in the spare seat opposite Shaw and launched into a cheerful description of Ouaisne Bay. Noting the look on Shaw's face, he paused. 'Are you all right?'

'Not really,' Shaw answered, and found himself telling the whole story to Beck who listened with an expression of shock.

' . . . so that's it, really. No one has seen Ben since Wednesday. No one who's telling, that is,' he finished.

'I'm so sorry, Nick. What a thing to happen!' Beck exclaimed. 'Is there anything I can do to help?'

'Thanks for the offer, but at the moment I don't have any ideas.'

'Do you think the police are any good — I mean, are they doing enough?'

Shaw considered the question before answering. 'I'm not sure. I don't know if they would have got the extra information from George Bisson if I hadn't gone to see him.'

'No! He might never have told them.' Beck nodded vigorously. 'What do you think made him decide to talk to you?'

Shaw had been wondering about that himself. 'I think he was already worrying about Ben, and about the half-truths he had told to the police. My turning up just gave him an extra push.'

'You said there's going to be something in the newspaper tomorrow about this?' Beck asked.

'Yes, and on the local TV news.'

'Well. That might push someone else,' Beck suggested. He looked hard at Shaw, noting the pale, drawn face. 'Stop thinking the worst. Your friend might have gone off to France or one of the other islands. There might be a normal reason why no message has reached you. If so, you could well get a response from the news appeal.'

'Yes, that could be true,' Shaw conceded. 'I hope to God it's something like that. The problem is that Ben's been so excited about this, he *could* have done something stupid.'

'Okay, we'll think about that next, but

first we need a drink.' Beck left for the bar and returned a few minutes later with two pints.

'So. Ben left the coastguard's house after ten o'clock on Wednesday. Could he have gone back to Harry Scadden's house?'

'Yes. Particularly if he thought the police would've left. Maybe he would have gone to look for a hidden route down to Fliquet Bay, or for the place where Scadden was keeping the drugs.'

'Right. He could've seen someone else there who also had no legitimate reason to be searching the grounds. Maybe he followed them?'

'If it was Scadden's murderer or another smuggler, they would probably kill him if they spotted him,' Shaw said, feeling sick.

Beck shook his head. 'Not necessarily. If I were them, I'd want to find out what the nosy reporter knew first — and surely Ben would be able to say something to keep himself alive, giving the police time to find him.'

'Perhaps. He would certainly try.'

'And how about the chance that he followed someone and wasn't seen? He could be getting the story of his career right now. If he's hiding somewhere, watching the smugglers, would he risk having his phone go off?'

'You're determined to be optimistic aren't you?' Shaw accused Beck, but he could not help but smile a little. The man's enthusiasm was lifting his spirits. Ben had only been gone for two days, and it could still be all right. Perhaps Ben had sent a text that never got through and then turned his phone off for safety.

They talked for the best part of an hour, and the conversation gradually turned to lighter topics. Ryland was never far from Shaw's mind, but it was a relief to be diverted, and they walked back to the hotel discussing football.

Agreeing to ask Beck if he needed any help, Shaw started for the stairs when the desk clerk hurried towards him.

'Mr Shaw. There was a gentleman asking for you a short while ago. He didn't leave his name or a message.'

'What did he look like?' Shaw asked eagerly.

'Smart, sort of distinguished. Greying hair at the temples, slight tan. Probably about fifty, I'd guess.'

Shaw's momentary hope that it had been Ryland faded away, but his curiosity was aroused. The description did not match anyone he had met so far on Jersey.

'Can you call me immediately if he comes back?'

'Of course, sir.'

'Good. Did you tell the police about him?'

'No, sir. I've been very busy. Do you think I should?'

'Well, as I hardly know anyone here and he doesn't sound familiar, I can only suppose that there must be some link with Mr Ryland's disappearance.' Shaw tried to contain his annoyance. The clerk could only have been twenty years old at the most. 'I know it's getting late, but there will be someone at the station. Call them now.'

He found himself yawning. The stress

was definitely affecting his energy levels. He thought for a moment. There was no need for him to stay to talk with whichever officer got the message, and he strongly doubted if Raven himself would turn up.

Reasoning that if he was needed they could always call him, he went up to his room and flopped onto the bed and let his eyes close for a minute.

Several hours later, he woke, and sleepily undressed before sliding back into bed.

* * *

Saturday morning brought rain. The fine weather gave way to cloudier skies, and the light breezes of the day before had evolved into a definite wind. Shaw had walked down to the harbour's edge and was staring out to sea, watching the waves.

He had not been woken during the night, although the desk clerk had left him a message to say that the police had been informed of his visitor. Looking at

106

his watch, he saw it was nearly nine o'clock.

He was tempted to go round to the police station and see if Raven was available, so began to walk in that direction. A newsagent's shop in the next street caught his eye and he bought a copy of the *Jersey Evening Post*.

A covered bus stop gave him shelter from the rain which had settled into an annoying drizzle. A few pages in, he found an article about Ryland's disappearance and quickly read it through.

The police had given little away. They had said that there could be a connection between Ryland and the death of Harry Scadden, but had left out most of the details. There was a good photograph of Ryland, and of a car like the one he had hired, and it was possible that the car at least could be found. *Unless it's been dumped in one of Jersey's reservoirs*, Shaw thought gloomily.

He was finding it harder and harder to avoid the possibility that Ryland was dead. He folded up the paper and was about to leave the shelter when a man walked in.

'Mr Shaw, I believe?' the stranger said.

Shaw looked round and saw a well-dressed man in his late fifties. The clothes were a cut above anything Shaw could afford, and the overall effect was of wealth and confidence. Looking more closely at the man's face, however, he had an idea that the confidence was a little forced.

He also had a strong suspicion that he knew who this man must be.

'Yes, and I would guess that you're Dominic Harland,' he answered.

Harland nodded and then dodged out of reach as Shaw made a grab for him. 'Hold on a minute!' he said.

'No! You're seeing the police right now.'

Shaw tried again to get a hold on Harland, but pulled up short as the older man drew a knife from his pocket.

'I may well go to the police, but on my own terms,' Harland said forcefully. 'I want to know how things stand.'

He slid the knife up his sleeve until it was only just visible.

'We'll have a quiet talk here and then

I'll leave you in peace.'

Shaw did not believe a word of it, but Harland had looked very familiar with the weapon and he could not see how to get it away from him.

'Okay, say what you have to.'

'Is it true that Ben Ryland has been missing since I saw him on Wednesday night?'

'Yes.'

'And there's been no word from him or any sightings at all?'

'Nothing.'

'And you've been in contact with the police about this?'

'Of course I have! DCI Raven is working on it, and he wants to speak with you urgently.'

'He's the one on the Scadden murder as well,' Harland said, almost to himself. 'Do you think Raven suspects me in either case?'

Shaw thought hard. He really did not know what line Raven was taking, but he wanted to get Harland to talk to the police whatever the truth was. 'I doubt it,' he answered. 'I think he's more interested in whether you've any information about Scadden or Ben.'

Harland paused, weighing up Shaw's answers.

Tired of waiting, Shaw blurted out: '*Did* you have anything to do with Ben vanishing?'

'No. That wasn't the idea at all. He was going to help me put pressure on someone else,' Harland answered somewhat absently, then pulled himself together. 'Where do you fit into all this, anyway? Are you a journalist too?'

Shaw shook his head. 'I'm a travel writer. Ben suggested we come here so that I could do a write-up on Jersey while he worked on the smuggling story.'

'Have you heard of Samuel Curzon or Dave Damerell?' Harland demanded, watching Shaw intently.

'No!' Shaw retorted. 'Who the hell are they?'

'Damerell runs a very tight group of people on the south coast of England. People who can get hold of most things that wouldn't make it through customs. Curzon works for him, and his specialist skill is the art of persuasion — by any means necessary.' Harland had taken to fingering the tip of his knife, and was looking warily along the street by the bus shelter.

'I spotted him over on the north coast on Thursday morning. Damerell must have sent him to take out Scadden. The chances of it being a coincidence are just too small. I thought it had been Scadden's second-in-command who decided to kill him and take over. That would have been fine, we could have got him under our thumb easily enough, but Damerell is a different matter.'

'How do you know all this?' Shaw asked, trying to keep all the names straight in his head. He was also looking for any opening that would allow him to overpower Harland. The possibility of being knifed seemed all too real.

'I used to work for Damerell, years ago. Curzon was just a runner back then, but he soon made himself useful. He looks perfectly normal, but he's a vicious bastard underneath. Christ! I'm going to have to go to Raven, ask for protection. If

Curzon spots me he'll definitely try to kill me, just for old times' sake.'

Shaw felt a surge of relief. Harland probably knew more than he had divulged so far, and if he was willing to talk to the police, he could swap the information he possessed for leniency.

'Do you know anything that might help us find Ben? I mean, do you think he's in danger from Curzon?'

'God, I don't know. He doesn't usually kill people unless there's a good reason; and unfortunately, he has a good reason with me. If Ben got close to something they want to keep under wraps, then he'd put the frighteners on him, but Damerell doesn't like random violence.' Harland's eyes narrowed as he remembered something.

'Although . . . Ben did say something that struck me as odd, just after we left George's house. He asked me how long I thought it would take for someone to get Scadden's route working smoothly again. Now, back then, I thought Larry Baker was the most likely suspect to have bumped old Harry off, and I guessed that he would keep everything quiet until the police had lost interest.

'I told him it doesn't take long: a few months, usually, if the right palms are greased. Ben looked worried about that and said something like, 'How risky would it be to do a few more runs? Surely the police won't cotton on to the mechanics of the trade so quickly. Okay, Scadden's out of it but there must be other beaches and coves that a couple of boats can meet up at.'

'He seemed to be very anxious that the route should stay open.' Harland looked appraisingly at Shaw. 'My instinct told me that I'd work well with Ben, and that's not exactly a glowing recommendation.'

Shaw began to feel his fists itching. Harland was just the kind of smooth, selfish manipulator that he hated. 'You met Ben only once. Don't judge him by your standards.'

'Don't be naïve. I want to know exactly what he was doing here. I thought George had just found a bright-eyed journo, but there's something different about him.' Harland continued to glance worriedly up and down the street. 'Has he got his own ideas? Has he told you anything?'

'For God's sake, Ben's a reporter! He wants the best story possible. There's nothing else to it,' Shaw retorted hotly.

Harland gave him a pitying look. 'Yes, and George Bisson is just a good citizen,' he said sarcastically. 'I suppose what really concerns me is keeping out of Curzon's way. He hasn't seen me yet, and I intend to keep it that way. I take it this Inspector Raven is based at the Rouge Bouillon station?'

'Yes,' Shaw snapped tersely.

'I may pay him a visit. Oh, and I'd advise you not to follow me. I have one or two things to take care of first, and I really object to having someone traipsing along after me.' He let the knife show in his hand again. 'You wouldn't want to have a regrettable accident.'

So saying, he walked briskly out of the bus shelter.

Shaw watched furiously as Harland turned down a side street and vanished from sight. Making up his mind to at least get an idea of where the blackmailer was going, he ran over, and was just in time to see him cross a busy road and go into one of the main shopping areas. A moment later, he was gone.

Shaw scanned the area, but there were too many possible exits to narrow it down and he was left fuming. The only useful thing he could think of was to call Raven.

He got through almost immediately, and then followed Raven's stern instruction to stay where he was and wait for the police.

An impatient ten minutes later, Shaw was still waiting. The distant wail of a siren started up and drew closer, only to stop a little way off. Puzzled, he looked around for any sign of Raven or uniformed officers, but there were none visible.

Then an ambulance rounded the corner, its siren almost deafening. It went further along the street and Shaw broke into a run, following it.

The traffic was impeding the progress of the ambulance, and he caught it easily when it turned again and came to a halt by a ring of people and a few police.

He pushed his way through, and saw Raven crouched beside the bloody body of Dominic Harland.

6

The interview room at the police station was rapidly getting on Shaw's nerves, and the weak coffee he was sipping left a lot to be desired. Necessary though he knew it was to go over his meeting with Harland, he was eager to get it over with and Raven had been delayed.

At last the door opened and Raven walked in, clutching a mug of his own. 'Sorry to keep you waiting. It's turned into a hell of a morning,' he said, taking the chair opposite Shaw.

'I can confirm that Mr Harland died in the ambulance on the way to the hospital. He didn't regain consciousness, so there are no deathbed confessions to help us out. I need to know what he told you in as much detail as you can possibly remember.'

'But how did he die? Was it a hit and run?' Shaw asked.

He had been hustled away from the

body and into a police car as soon as they had seen him. Whether to protect him, or because they suspected him, he had no idea.

'No. We do have a witness — a shop owner who was staring out the window in a quiet moment. She says that Harland was walking briskly along the street when another man came up behind him. The stranger put his hand on Harland's shoulder in what she thought was a friendly gesture, but then Harland crumpled to the ground and the stranger strode on.

'She ran out and saw a pool of blood spreading from his chest. He probably hit his head as he fell because he was unconscious when she reached him.

'The ambulance crew report that he had one very deep wound to the abdomen, angled upwards towards the heart. They tried to keep him going, but think he died of blood loss. We'll know more when they open him up.' Raven stopped, looking intently at Shaw. 'So what can you tell me?'

Shaw took a deep breath and went

methodically through the meeting as accurately as he could remember.

Raven listened and made notes, asking the occasional question but mostly letting Shaw speak. After Shaw reached the point where he saw Harland lying on the ground, Raven sat back in his chair with a sigh.

'Well, if Harland was telling you the truth, it's pretty clear that he was assassinated, quite possibly by this Samuel Curzon. Whether it was for past actions or for his involvement in the Scadden business, I don't know. Are you sure that you didn't see anyone watching you at the bus stop?'

'Positive. Harland can't have seen anyone either, and he was looking out almost all the time.'

'Then hopefully the killer didn't see you together. I've put everyone I can onto spotting this man, and there should be something on the CCTV camera for that area. The centre of the town's well-covered. According to the witness, though, the man wore a rain-jacket with the hood up, so we might not see much.

It was a blatant attack, but a very professional one. It certainly fits in with what Harland told you about Curzon being an enforcer for Damerell.'

'Have you heard of him before, then? Damerell, I mean,' Shaw asked. He gave up on his coffee and pushed the mug away.

'I hadn't until last week. When Mr Ryland came to see us, he talked about a leading smuggler on the south coast of England, although he claimed not to have any names. A few calls to my colleagues over there turned up several possibilities, with David Damerell topping the list. It could well be that a falling-out between him and Scadden resulted in Curzon being dispatched to get rid of the Jersey upstart. There's seldom any love lost between criminals. Whether I'll be able to prove it is another matter, of course.'

Shaw nodded. He had been thinking much the same.

'You're probably right. To be honest, I don't give a damn about Scadden and Harland, but surely there must be something else you can do to find Ben?'

The image of Harland, stripped of all his swagger and dying on the pavement, had heightened his fears for Ryland's safety. 'What about the guy Harland mentioned — Larry Baker? He worked with Scadden, and there must be others. How come you don't *know* these things?'

Raven looked away, his eyes trained on the far wall of the room. 'I can understand your frustration and your worries, Mr Shaw,' he said evenly. 'I'm not at liberty to discuss every aspect of the investigation with you, but please believe that we are following up all the possibilities. I realise that this is putting a great deal of stress on you, particularly as you're here on your own.'

'My wellbeing is not the problem here, Raven. Ben's is,' Shaw replied curtly.

The shock of Harland's death was turning into anger at the police. Raven seemed to have achieved nothing at all, and the only breaks had come to him via Shaw himself. He clenched his teeth, trying to resist the urge to rail at Raven for his lack of progress.

The tense moment of silence was

broken by a knock on the interview room door.

Raven cleared his throat and said: 'Come in.'

'Excuse me, sir,' a uniformed police-woman apologised. 'Could I have a quick word?'

'Of course,' Raven said, rising from his seat. 'I think we've gone over everything for now, Mr Shaw, but I'd be grateful if you could stay to check and sign your statement. It shouldn't take long.' He left the room without waiting for an answer.

Shaw spent the next quarter of an hour retelling his encounter with Harland to an officer who painstakingly went over every detail with him. At the end, Shaw signed it, and was asked to wait until the officer had checked with Raven that he could go.

Shaw looked at his watch and frowned to see that it was already nearly eleven o'clock. He had been in the station for over an hour and was in need of a break. He had declined the offer of another coffee but accepted the chocolate digestive, and had brought out his travel notebook. He was flicking through the pages, trying to distract himself, when Raven finally appeared.

'I'm sorry for the delay, Mr Shaw, but we've caught Curzon!' Raven's eyes were gleaming. 'A real stroke of luck for once. We put out an alert as soon as we found Harland, and one of our officers spotted a man matching the description near the ferry terminal. She sent for backup and we got him.'

'That's brilliant!' Shaw exclaimed. 'He *must* have something to do with Ben disappearing. Do you think you can make him talk?'

'Well, I'm damn well going to try,' Raven answered. 'It can be tricky with professional criminals, but there should be some leverage to do with his knowledge of Damerell's organisation. Faced with a charge of two murders and one abduction, he may be willing to help.'

He reined in his obvious excitement at catching Curzon, and said more sombrely: 'I'm hopeful that we might find out what has happened to Mr Ryland, but I have to say I'm not as hopeful that it will be good news.'

Shaw nodded briskly. 'I know, but from what Harland said, there were strong reasons why Curzon might kill him and Scadden. There can't have been as much reason to do away with Ben.'

'True. I'll be taken up with interviewing Curzon for the moment, and you can go now. With him off the streets, there's no need for us to keep you here.'

'Is that what was going on?' Shaw asked, but he was not really surprised; and if he was honest with himself, the thought that Curzon might have been watching the station for his departure had crossed his mind more than once.

'Just a precaution. As you've pointed out, professionals tend not to kill unless they're sure it's necessary.'

Raven walked Shaw to the exit and bade him goodbye, promising to keep him updated.

On the steps of the station, Shaw hesitated, not sure what to do with himself. He was half-tempted to hang around the station in the hope of seeing a fleet of cars speed off, acting on information about Ryland. What he would do if that happened was another matter, of course.

Deciding it was pointless staying, he headed for a nearby park and found a quiet place to sit while he called Louisa. Her personal mobile was, unsurprisingly, turned off, so he left a brief message.

It felt like there was nothing more he could do, and he did not want to just wait in the hotel. Raven could contact him anywhere on his phone, and if he was needed, there was nowhere on the island that took long to drive back from.

He took out his map to look at the north coast — the only area he had not touched yet. There was no obvious coastal route, but the challenge of picking his way through the small, winding roads might take his mind off things. Whenever he sat still he felt the apprehension steadily getting worse.

What if Ben had been dead for days — or, even worse, what if they were only just too late?

No. It was no good sitting around. He folded up the map and returned to the hotel just long enough to get the car.

Then he turned out and headed west to pick up La Route de Beaumont.

Unseen by him, a small silver car that had been parked near the *Pomme d'Or* nosed out into the traffic and set off behind him.

Half an hour later, Shaw pulled onto the grass verge to admire the view over the cliffs. A crunch of gravel behind him prompted him to turn round, and he saw a woman approach him with a map.

'Could you show me where we are? I'm a little lost,' she asked, apologetically.

'Of course,' Shaw replied, and bent his head over the map. A hard blow on the back of his head sent him sprawling to the ground.

* * *

'Nick! Wake up!'

Shaw heard the words as a vague mumble, somewhere far away. They could not possibly refer to him, so he let himself sink back into unconsciousness.

The man kneeling beside him grunted

in exasperation and pulled himself up, using the camp bed to support himself. He reached for a bottle of water and tipped a little into his hand, brought it to Shaw's face, and wiped it over his forehead.

The cold water had some effect, and he tried again.

'Come on, Nick. Wake up for God's sake!' the man said, shaking Shaw gently.

There was a deeper intake of breath, and then Shaw slowly opened his eyes.

'Thank God! Now, stay with me this time, Nick, or Louisa will have my hide for a hearthrug.'

Shaw tried hard to focus his eyes and get his brain working.

There was not a lot to see in the dim light, so he gave up on that and let his mind slowly comprehend the sounds he was hearing. His eyes snapped open.

'Ben?' he said, disbelievingly.

'That took a while. Yes, it's me,' Ryland replied. 'No, don't sit up just yet. You got hit on the head.'

'What's going on, Ben? Why didn't you

answer your phone?' Shaw asked. He could not quite remember everything, but he knew he had been trying to call Ryland. There seemed to be cotton wool between his ears, and he felt a strange reluctance to think about it.

Ryland regarded Shaw with his lop-sided smile, although it looked forced. 'Believe me, I would've answered it if I could, Nick. I've been stuck here for days. I haven't seen you since Wednesday, and I think it's Saturday now. It's easy to lose track of the days down here.'

'Down here?' Shaw asked. He could make out an uneven floor and rough walls. There was a weak lightbulb hanging from the ceiling with a wire trailing over to a closed door. 'Where are we?'

'It's a kind of cave. There's the door just here, and when I followed the path over there — ' Ryland pointed to one corner. ' — I got to a locked metal gate, but there's only the sea beyond it.'

Shaw realised that he had been smelling seawater since he came round. With Ryland's help, he gingerly sat up.

His head hurt, but it was bearable and

he felt better upright — less helpless. Some of the cotton wool was dissipating, and as it did, more memories came back to him.

'Have some water, it might help,' Ryland said, handing Shaw the bottle. 'You've been here about half an hour.'

'Ben, what the hell is going on? I remember driving out to the coast, and then there's just nothing there. Raven said he'd got Curzon. It should have been safe!'

'What! How do you know about Curzon?' Ryland exclaimed. 'Raven? That's the detective, isn't it?'

Shaw sighed, closed his eyes and began to talk, going over everything he could remember from the time Ryland had vanished.

' ... So I guess Raven must have arrested the wrong person, or I wouldn't be here now.'

Ryland sat in silence for a few more moments, then finally spoke. 'Trust the police to get confused, at least as far as my disappearance is concerned. Curzon wouldn't be any threat to me — or to you, for that matter. Christ, Nick, I'm really sorry you've been caught up in this.'

Shaw opened his eyes.

Ryland was hunched on the floor looking wretched.

'I don't understand. It wasn't Curzon who put you here?'

'No. If we're lucky, he might be able to give the police some idea of where to look for us, but I wouldn't count on it. Okay, I'd better start at the beginning.

'You know that Harry Scadden was running drugs from the European mainland to Britain, among other places? Well, he'd been working with Dave Damerell. Harland had that right. Scadden thought he should have a bigger share of the profits, and started to keep certain deals back from Damerell. He was only a small-time criminal, but he had ideas above his station.

'It came to a head about a month ago, when Scadden brokered a very lucrative deal with one of his contacts in France, and was intending to cut Damerell out completely. Someone must have talked, because Curzon must have been despatched to take Scadden out of the running. He's been hanging around, keeping an eye on things over here. I recognised him that first night at the hotel.'

'So *he* hanged Harry Scadden? But why did he kill Harland, and why are you saying it wasn't him who put you here?' Shaw asked, trying to follow the story.

'Curzon didn't get to him in time,' Ryland said. 'It turns out Scadden was killed by a man called Larry Baker.'

Shaw looked up more alertly. 'Harland mentioned him!'

'Baker was Scadden's first mate, you could say. Worked with him for years until Scadden made a bad mistake. Baker's a brilliant sailor and he planned all the routes, recruited most of the crews, and kept them all ahead of the police and the coastguards. In fact, it was Baker that poor old George Bisson was tracking most of the time. He'd be out in all weathers while Scadden did all the negotiations and bribery. There's been a lot of that going round on the islands, and

131

it's been driving Bisson mad.

'Anyway, Baker was happy with the system until the day that his wife told him Scadden kept propositioning her. He'd turn up when he knew Baker was out on a run, and he was getting more persistent. Within a week of Baker finding out, Scadden was swinging from a beam — ahead of Damerell's schedule. I imagine Curzon wasn't happy about that.'

'So Baker killed Scadden, just like Harland suspected?' Shaw exclaimed.

'Yes. Harland knew a lot more than he ever told Bisson. If he'd been an honest man and gone to the police earlier, he might have been alive today; although from what I've heard, his card was marked a long time ago.'

'God, my head hurts.' Shaw found the pain was sharpening as his brain cleared. He suddenly patted his pocket. 'Where's my phone?' he asked.

'It wasn't on you when Baker brought you here. I checked. He has mine too — if he hasn't already smashed it, that is.'

'Makes sense, I suppose,' Shaw said.

'So it was Larry Baker who got you too. How?'

'After I had that meeting with George Bisson and Dominic Harland, I was walking back to my car when Harland came after me. He offered to tell me where Scadden stored his goods, and I said 'yes'.

'He said that he wouldn't come along, but he could direct me to the cave entrance to the north, and that it was easy in daylight. I think he didn't want to be the one to risk his own skin investigating it.'

Ryland was absent-mindedly twisting the cuff of his jumper with his fingers.

'So you hared off there at night, on your own,' Shaw stated flatly. 'Ben, that was really — '

'Stupid,' Ryland interrupted. 'Actually, I haven't got to the really stupid bit.' He shifted uncomfortably on the stone floor and winced.

'As you're upright now, can I have your pillow?' he asked, and when Shaw passed it down he propped it under his left leg. 'I wrenched my knee when Baker caught me and it's not getting any better. I really wanted to see Scadden's store, and I convinced myself it was an easy job, so I drove in the direction of the quarry and found the side road that Harland had marked on my map. It was just as he described it: a small house near the cliff edge, and a pathway a little way off, with *Private* signs everywhere.

'There were no lights on in the house, and there would have been if anyone was home as it was about half-past ten. So I sneaked down the path where it led past the house, and it soon sloped downward towards the sea. It was almost pitch-black and my torch wasn't much good.

'I could just make out the opening of a cave, so I hurried forward and ran straight into a man coming out of the entrance.'

'Baker?' Shaw asked.

'Yes, although I didn't know him at the time. The really worrying thing was that he knew *me*.'

Shaw frowned. 'How's that possible?'

'It took me a while to work it out, and I still don't know all the details, but he certainly recognised me.' Ryland shook his head in annoyance.

'Baker just grabbed hold of me before I could react. I felt a knife against my ribs and he took me up to the house. He and his wife went through everything I had on me. They took my phone, my wallet, everything. Then he started asking questions: Was I really a reporter? How much did I know? What did Damerell want, and why had Curzon been sent over?'

'How would he expect you to know that?' Shaw asked, incredulously.

'Because he recognised me from a night two months ago. I was on a fishing boat, helping to transfer bags from the boat he was piloting. It was pretty dark and I didn't get a good look at him then, but I suppose he's more used to those conditions, or he's got good night vision.' Ryland sighed. 'This is where I get to the really stupid bit.' He shuffled across the floor until his back was against the wall.

'When I started to research smuggling, I had this idea for a great exposé that would damn the smugglers and the police alike. I'd talked to a couple of press liaison officers, but they didn't want to give me much information.

'Then I started looking for the criminal side of the story. It took a while, and it was mostly in my own time, but eventually I got to know some guys in the middle of the supply chain.'

'You mean dealers?' Shaw asked bluntly.

'Yes, the ones who actually get their products from Damerell's operation. He doesn't run dealers himself, he doesn't need to. I was pretty upfront about why I was interested, and some of them were so cocky that they liked the idea of being interviewed on an 'all names will be changed' basis.

'There were others who were a lot more wary, though; one time I turned up to talk with a guy, and a couple more sort of materialised from the nearby streets. It was the middle of the night, and when they suggested that I should meet a friend of theirs, I didn't really have a choice. That's when I met Dave Damerell.

'He didn't like the way I was snooping around his affairs, and I was getting more and more scared and talking more and more rubbish. I went on about how much I admired the skill and daring needed to get away with smuggling.' Ryland had been mostly talking to the floor, but he looked up now, and his wry smile was self-mocking.

'You once said that I was like a modern version of the plucky young reporter from a black and white film. Well, I played the part of 'easily-led young idiot' for all I was worth. When I finally ran out of things to say, Damerell just looked at me for what felt like an age. Then he said that he might have a deal for me.'

'Oh God, Ben! What the hell did you agree to?' Shaw said, his heart sinking.

'Not much!' Ryland insisted. 'I had to get out of there alive, and all he wanted was for me to go along on a pick-up. He said that if I really wanted to understand the business, I should get an idea of what was involved. No, wait!' he said as Shaw groaned and started to interrupt. 'Let me tell you it all. They were going out the next night to collect a delivery from Scadden, and I was to accompany two of

Damerell's men in the boat. Of course I said yes! You would have too. I was going to leg it to the police the moment I was out of there. The trouble was that I never got to leave. They kept me there all the next day, and Damerell started to tell me about the problems he was having with Harry Scadden. He'd got this idea to set Scadden up and make it really public.

'You see, Damerell keeps his head down. All his assets are off-shore in more ways than one. The way he sees it is that he'll have enough money in a few more years to leave Britain for good and never get his hands dirty again. Until that day, he doesn't buy flash cars or live in luxury. He's very controlled.

'Scadden was a different kind of man. He had a legitimate business that he'd made a fortune with, but he always wanted more, and he liked taking risks. When I got the chance to do some research on him, I found photo after photo of him with politicians or minor celebrities, even giving large hand-outs to charities.

'When Damerell realised that Scadden

was cheating him, he wanted revenge, and that meant exposing Scadden to all of his VIP friends.' He paused and took a drink of water.

'So is that where you would come in?' Shaw asked. His head was still throbbing, but he tried to force himself to think clearly. Ryland's tale was all too miserably believable, and he was struggling not to get angry. Just the thought of getting upset made his headache worse.

'Yes. I don't know if he would have gone through with it in the end, but he certainly wanted to explore the idea of me dragging Scadden's name through the mud. How he thought I could do it without bringing in his own set-up, I don't know. But he's the kind of man who just demands you do things the way he wants; and if that's problematic, well, it's your problem, not his.

'So I had to go out with the others, and we sailed to a point just north of Alderney where we met Larry Baker, except he stayed in the cabin bit of the boat while we unloaded the goods. He would have been able to see me far better than I could see him. We went back to Damerell's base and they watched me all the time. One of them was quite talkative and it was he who told me about Harland, as a cautionary tale.'

'I've been wondering about his part in all of this. What did you find out about him?' Shaw asked.

'Harland was originally Damerell's man. He's a linguist, so he went on a lot of trips to Europe with Damerell, and then later without him. It was on one of these that he decided to go it alone and never came back to England. The chatty guy said that Damerell had put out a kill-on-sight order on Harland. That must be what happened to him when Curzon found him.'

Ryland shifted his leg, trying to find a more comfortable position. 'How Harland thought he was safe, this close to Damerell, I don't know.'

'Even when he was scared enough to go to the police, he was still arrogant.'

'He was an idiot, but who am I to talk?' Ryland muttered.

'Ben, I can understand how you got

suckered into going on that pick-up, but how did it all get to *this* point? Damerell obviously let you go in the end, so why didn't you go to the police, just tell them everything?' Shaw could not keep the frustration out of his voice.

'Fear, for the most part,' Ryland finally answered. 'Then a certain amount of avarice.'

'Avarice? Was Damerell paying you?' Shaw asked incredulously.

'After the pick-up, I was taken to see Damerell again, and he told me what I was going to do. And I mean *told*. He'd give me the inside information to totally discredit Scadden; I, being a law-abiding citizen, would present it to the police, and then later get the chance to make a lot of money from the story. I thought I was getting off lightly. I was tired from the night's work, and scared of what might happen, but it seemed like I'd get out of it alive and with what I had wanted in the first place.'

'What was the catch? There had to have been one.'

'Damerell's insurance policy was the

catch. If I tried to cross him, go to the police or just not do the job, he would bring to their attention a large payment he had transferred to my account. He also had video evidence that I'd taken part in smuggling heroin into Britain, and plenty of people who would swear blind that I'd been doing it for months. On the other hand, if I kept my mouth shut and followed orders, I could keep the money, get the story, and that would be the end of it.'

'Oh, come on! Did you really believe that?' Shaw exclaimed, angrily. 'Someone like that would never let you off the hook!'

'I know that!' Ryland replied. 'I'm not that stupid. I was exhausted and had been expecting a bullet half the night! All I could think was that if I said 'yes' he'd let me go. It's not as if I was signing up to kill someone!'

'Two people have ended up dead though, Ben,' Shaw said.

'It's not my fault!' Ryland retorted. 'Larry Baker killed Scadden, and Harland was dead meat from the moment he left

Damerell.' He was fidgeting; whether with pain from his knee, or anger, Shaw did not know.

'I was glad to get away. You would have been too. When I got home my flat had been broken into. Not trashed or anything, but the lock had been forced, and someone had tracked mud into my bedroom. Damerell's way of letting me know that I had nowhere to hide. Don't you see, Nick? I had to at least look like I was falling into line.'

'What do you mean, 'look like'?' Shaw asked sharply.

'I've been wrestling with this ever since that night. I needed to get away from him, and I'd worked out how to do it. That's why I asked you to come with me.'

'Why on earth *did* you get me involved with this?' Shaw demanded angrily.

'Because of Louisa,' Ryland answered.

Shaw drew a sharp intake of breath, and was about to demand an explanation when they both heard footsteps coming towards the door.

7

Ryland and Shaw looked anxiously at the opening door.

A man came in with a plastic bag in one hand and a nasty-looking knife in the other.

'Food,' he said abruptly, dropping the bag on the floor. He looked at Shaw appraisingly. 'You've come round, then. I'll tell you what I told him. I'll send someone to let you go once the cargo is safely on its way. It won't matter what you do then.'

'Cargo?' Shaw asked, trying to look more confused than he felt. He wanted to get the measure of Baker while appearing befuddled.

'Ask your friend. He knows all about it,' Baker replied. He looked at Ryland and said with some satisfaction: 'Damerell's not going to like my version of the story you know. Do you want to change your mind?'

Ryland mutely shook his head.

Baker shrugged and gestured at Shaw. 'How's he doing?' he asked Ryland.

'Still pretty out of it,' Ryland replied, taking his cue from Shaw.

Baker took one last look at both of his captives and left, locking the door behind him.

Ryland grabbed the bag and unpacked it. 'Bread rolls, ham, water; same as last time, just more of it.' He shared out the supplies and started to eat.

'Ben, what's the cargo, and what haven't you changed your mind about? And what was that about Louisa?' Shaw exclaimed. 'What have you got me into?'

'I'm sorry. I promise I didn't think you'd be in any danger.'

'You should have told me what was going on!' Shaw insisted. 'I don't like being taken for a fool.'

'You'd have told me to go straight to the police, wouldn't you?' Ryland said, between bites.

'Too right I would! You were stupid, and there would've been a lot of difficult questions, but all the information you had about Damerell would've got you out of any custodial sentence. Louisa could have told you that if you'd asked.'

'I had information, yes, but not evidence. It would be my word against theirs and Damerell would get to hear of it, you can be sure of that. I wouldn't get anything like police protection. Not without proof,' Ryland said.

'I don't think you're right about that, and you could have run it by her: said you were asking for another person, or just for research,' Shaw retorted. 'You could have lied. It seems you're good at that.'

'It wasn't supposed to happen like this!' Ryland insisted. 'Just listen, will you? Damerell told me to get myself over to Jersey and find out anything I could about Scadden, as a reporter. When I found out he was dead, I could hardly believe it. I thought Damerell had changed his mind and killed him instead, but that didn't seem to fit. Then I got a message from him telling me to stay put and await orders.' He broke off to take a swig of water.

'I decided to do some investigating on

my own. If I could get hard evidence against the whole lot of them, it would be worth it. George Bisson has a lot I could use, and he's willing to testify to it. He'd be a credible witness, even with his past. Harland was no good on that front, of course.'

'What was that about Bisson's past? Harland hinted at something too,' Shaw asked.

'I forgot you don't know. When he started to suspect Scadden and Baker, George hid at Fliquet Bay one night, hoping to catch them in the act. He heard Baker joking with another man about the coastguards being a waste of taxpayers' money, and he lost his temper. He tried to run them over. Clipped one man, not Baker, and tried to reverse for a second go. Baker stopped him, punched his lights out, and the next thing George knew, it was morning.

'He went to the police, but no one believed him. He had alcohol in his system, and the bruises looked like he had hit his head on the steering wheel. Baker had a dozen alibis. There were no traces of anything illegal found at any of Scadden's properties, and George came over like an embittered drunk who made a mistake.'

'Christ, he must have hated that,' Shaw said. 'But if you found evidence to back up his claim, everything would be different. No wonder he was so keen to recruit you!'

'Exactly. If I found a stash of drugs at Baker's cave, or any of the paraphernalia of drug dealing, George would be the wronged hero of the piece, finally vindicated. I'd have done what Damerell wanted and be home free, *and* I'd have a bloody good story to boost my career.'

Ryland had some of his old enthusiasm back, to Shaw's increasing annoyance. He opened his mouth to continue, but Shaw interrupted.

'Instead of which, you got caught, injured, and imprisoned. You also got *me* caught and I can't see any prospect of getting out of here. Face it, Ben, you screwed up. Now, stop avoiding the question and tell me where Louisa fits into it.'

'Okay,' Ryland said, the excited gleam in his eyes vanishing once more. 'I'd put something in place as a sort of insurance against Damerell — in case he tried to keep me under his thumb after the Scadden work had been done. He said once I'd done that for him he'd leave me alone, but I'm not stupid enough to believe that. I told him that if he tried to get rid of me, or to send the incriminating stuff he had made up to the police, I'd do the same to him. I said I had a friend in the police force who would get all the information I had amassed about him if anything happened to me.

'He just laughed and said it wouldn't do any good. He also said I didn't need to worry, just get on with the job. I was so scared when I came off the phone from him that time. I could see myself being thrown off one of his boats at night, or being pursued by Curzon wherever I went. I'd met him during that day they kept me captive, and I had no wish to repeat the experience.' He dropped his head, not meeting Shaw's eyes.

'I was going frantic trying to work out

what to do when I remembered you'd talked about doing a walking holiday or something together. I realised that if I had you with me on Jersey, it would look like I had a hotline to Louisa in case of trouble — maybe even make him think that you were the one in possession of the incriminating disk. Damerell could easily find out who you were and verify that I was telling him the truth.

'I thought it would keep him at arm's reach until I was ready to blow all of them out of the water. It sort of worked, too. I mean, it was Baker who did all of this, not Damerell.'

Shaw was almost lost for words. The idea that he had been used like that, been put in danger along with Louisa, was compounding the anger he already felt towards Ryland. If he had been feeling better, he would undoubtedly have hit him.

As it was, he still felt light-headed, and thought that if he took a swing at Ryland he would probably miss and fall over. He closed his eyes and tried to think of how he could get out of this mess.

'Nick? Say something, for God's sake!' Ryland finally broke the silence. 'I'm so sorry about all of this.'

'I'm not going to waste my energy shouting at you, Ben, but if we manage to survive this I don't want you anywhere near me or Louisa ever again,' Shaw answered coldly.

'I didn't know what else to do!' Ryland protested.

'You should've taken the risk and gone to the police right at the beginning, behaved like an adult for a change,' Shaw shot back. 'I don't want to hear more attempts at self-justification. All I want to do is get away from here. Any other subject is off-limits. Right, did you actually arrange for the information to be sent to Louisa?'

'Yes, but it won't have worked yet. I gave a disk to Rick to send on if I didn't check in with him after three days. I spoke to him on Wednesday, just before meeting up with Harland and Bisson, so he won't do anything until tomorrow. If I miss today's deadline, he should send it off.'

'And is there enough on there to lead her to this place?' Shaw asked, though he did not have much hope.

'Not really; not straight here, anyway. I added a bit about Baker before we came here, but I didn't know where he lived.'

'Okay, so it's not much good waiting to be rescued. She'll worry that I haven't been in touch by tonight, and she might well chase up Raven, but I don't know how much good he'll be — no one knew where I was going.'

Shaw hesitated. 'That's a point,' he murmured. 'Ben, did you tell anyone about me being here with you — besides Damerell I mean?'

'No, not a soul,' Ryland said, shaking his head in emphasis

'I know it came as a surprise to Bisson when I visited him, but Harland knew me. I suppose he talked with Bisson. But how would Larry Baker know who I was?'

'I think he was keeping watch on the hotel. He could have seen you with me and assumed we were working together. There would be no reason to snatch you otherwise. Can you remember anything about your abduction?' Ryland pressed him. 'It would've been Baker or his wife, I'd guess, or both together. I don't think he's let any of his other pilots in on this yet.'

Shaw tried hard to penetrate the strange blankness that seemed to surround his memory. He knew he had been driving along heading north, and he had passed a sign saying a*Maizin!* which stuck in his mind. A little later, he had driven through St Ouen and on to smaller roads. 'I think I was heading east along one of the most northerly routes.' He frowned. Fragments of memory were staying just out of reach.

'Was it sunny or dull? Did it rain?' Ryland asked

'Cloudy, I think. It certainly rained this morning. It might have been raining then.'

'Did you have the wipers on?'

Shaw concentrated hard. 'I . . . think so.'

'Okay, so you're driving in the rain, along a narrow road. Did something make you stop?'

'I'm not sure, Ben. It's too fuzzy.'

'Well, did you recognise Baker when he came in here?'

'Definitely not. I've never seen him before.'

'How about a woman? His wife's a brunette, quite tall and attractive. She looks a cut above Baker.'

Shaw felt a part of his mind clear. He did have a memory of a woman like that. He held up his hand to stop Ryland's next question. 'Be quiet a moment,' he said. Gradually, he let the memory form, not trying to force it this time.

'I'd got to a point where I could look down at the cliffs, so I parked up and walked. When I got back, there was another car there with a woman just like you described — willowy and well-dressed. I had the impression she was a tourist, though I don't know why. I think she made some comment about a map and I turned to look.'

He stopped as the memory came to an abrupt halt.

'I guess that either she or Baker slugged you about then,' Ryland said. 'You were pretty near his house, by the sounds of it. They probably thought that you had worked out where I was.'

Shaw felt slightly better at being able to remember now, although he still had a bad headache, and realised from the other pains in his body that he must have fallen heavily.

He carefully stood up. His legs were a bit wobbly, and his head seemed a lot further away from the ground than usual. He steadied himself on the rocky wall. 'I want to see this gate you mentioned.'

'Okay, but watch your step. It gets very dark at one point,' Ryland replied. He heaved himself up, putting as little weight on his leg as possible. 'Follow me.'

He led the way to the back of the cave and round a corner that Shaw had not noticed.

A rough-hewn stone corridor continued for several steps, getting darker every foot, and it was almost pitch-black before they turned the last corner and Shaw saw light ahead.

There was a new metal gate set into the rock. It was chained shut with a hefty padlock and the bars were set too close together to wriggle through. The path sloped downwards beyond the gate to the water, and there was a gap in the cave leading to the open sea about twenty feet from where they stood.

'This is one of Scadden's boltholes. Baker's now, I suppose,' Ryland explained, leaning against the wall to rest his leg. 'Bisson thinks the smugglers sometimes unload the larger boats at sea and bring the goods in by canoe to places like this.'

'Well, it's interesting, but not very helpful to us right now,' Shaw said, disappointed that there was no possible way out from there. 'Has Baker let you out of this room at all?'

'Yes, a couple of times a day to use the bathroom, which is a mercy I hadn't expected of him.'

'Probably doesn't want his nice clean cave messed up,' Shaw commented wryly. 'So do you think there's a chance of us overpowering him when he next comes in?'

'I doubt it. His wife comes too, and she has a gun. He does the unlocking and she keeps guard. If they carry on with that system, it would be very dangerous to try anything. I don't think we can get out of here by force, but I've been working on a different approach. There's nothing more to see here, Nick. Come back to the room.'

Shaw gave a last, regretful look at the locked gate and walked back, finding he was less wobbly this time. He chose to remain standing while Ryland gratefully took the camp bed for a seat. 'Okay, let's hear your plan, then.'

'Do you remember that Baker said he would let us go when the cargo was safe?' Ryland asked.

'Yes, and he asked if you'd changed your mind,' Shaw replied.

'That's right.' Ryland nodded. 'He told me that Scadden had been working to set up a new contact in France — a man who had access to top-quality cocaine and heroin. Scadden wanted to be in charge of the British end of the operation to distribute the drugs, not Damerell. He would've ended up even richer and far more powerful if it came off, but he was a fool to think Damerell would have let him get away with it.

'If Baker hadn't beaten him to it, Curzon would have been biding his time, working out the most satisfying way to kill Scadden, but he would've waited until the first delivery had been made. Then Damerell would be able to push Scadden out of the way and make a new deal with the European contact.'

'Why couldn't he do that anyway?'

'Because no one knows who he is. Damerell had caught wind of the deal, but he wasn't able to find out the details. Our kind host, Larry Baker, worked the practical side of things, and even he doesn't know who he or she is. The only information he has is that a boat called the *Ange de la Mer* will be meeting him between Jersey and France tonight for the exchange.

'Baker has the cash for the deal — he took it from Scadden's safe. His plan is to let whoever's on that boat know that the situation has changed but the deal is still on, only with a different broker.

Otherwise, he has no way of contacting the supplier.'

'So he wants to take over from Scadden?' Shaw said.

'Not entirely. Baker may be less knowledgeable than Scadden, but he's smarter. He knows what he can't do. His idea is to send the stuff to Damerell according to the usual arrangement, and with Scadden dead his cut will be higher anyway. The only problem he has is that he knows Damerell will be furious with him for killing Scadden. Damerell is territorial about retribution, and Baker definitely strayed onto his patch. If he turns up at the base in Devon with his new cargo, he could simply end up dead.'

Ryland looked up at Shaw with a wry smile. 'His solution is to send a go-between to take the flak. Someone who Damerell knows is already on his payroll.'

'That would be you, then, I take it?' Shaw asked, his heart sinking at how Ryland was getting dragged further into it all.

Ryland nodded. 'That's right. Seems

I'm everyone's gofer at the moment, or perhaps 'lemming' would be more accurate.'

'You can't agree to it, Ben,' Shaw said bluntly. 'He'll have to find someone else to put in the firing line.'

'I'd normally agree with you completely, but there are two things that are making me seriously consider it. Firstly, if I say yes he has to let me out of here — you too, if we play it right. Secondly, if I don't do it, he's planning to tell Damerell that I was trying to muscle in on the deal myself.'

Ryland's normal grin was twisted into a bitter, self-mocking grimace. 'I don't for a minute believe that Baker will let us go if we don't help him. If we're not useful, he's got little to lose by killing us, not now that he's already killed once; and even with Louisa on his trail, I don't think the police will find us in time — the cargo is sailing in tonight.'

Shaw stared at Ryland for a long moment. The three nights of imprisonment had taken their toll on him, and the boyish enthusiasm that everyone knew him for had waned to almost nothing. The anger Shaw felt was mixed with pity, but the anger was still winning.

If he were to get out of there alive, however, he would have to go along with Ryland's idea. Finally, he looked away, and picked up the bag of food that Baker had left. Fishing out a bread roll, he sat back down on the floor and tore a large chunk off it.

'All right. Before Baker asks for your final answer, tell me how you plan to work this. But the first chance we have, we're getting away from these bastards, okay? No heroics. No greed.'

Ryland nodded. 'We're going to have to be careful, though, and find the right moment. I can't make a run for it with my knee like this,' he said apologetically.

Shaw considered how badly Ryland had walked just going to the end of the tunnel. They were going to have to be both clever and lucky. The image of Harland, lying in a pool of blood on the pavement, kept intruding on his thoughts. It was time to plan.

8

Over an hour later, the door opened once more to reveal a woman standing in the corridor outside, a gun pointed towards them. Shaw immediately recognised her as the one who had chatted to him above the cliffs earlier that day.

'We want to speak to you. Come with me,' she said to Shaw. When Ryland also stood up, she shook her head. 'Only him. You stay here.'

Just as Ryland had guessed, Shaw thought. He followed her out of the room and found there was another door across the landing. According to Ryland, that was a toilet. Then there was a narrow staircase which he climbed ahead of his captor.

In the time since he had woken up, his headache had subsided to a level he could mostly ignore, although the low temperature and the damp air in the subterranean room had not helped his aching side, but he managed the stairs without too much difficulty.

At the top, there was an open door leading to a kitchen where Baker was seated at a table.

'Have a seat,' Baker said, indicating one of the empty chairs. He was a slim, wiry man with tanned skin and light brown hair. He looked like many of the boat owners Shaw had seen down at the harbour, although none of them had given the impression of cold-heartedness that Baker did.

Shaw sat down and concentrated on remembering the story that he and Ryland had decided upon. He opened his mouth to start talking, but Baker cut across him. 'How's the head?' he asked.

'Improving,' Shaw replied laconically.

'Melanie hit you a little too hard, but it's difficult to be accurate with these things.' Baker shrugged. 'Melanie! Find him some painkillers,' he called out. 'I want him to be able to think straight.'

While Melanie brought Shaw a couple of aspirin and a glass of water, Baker just sat still, watching Shaw appraisingly.

For his part, Shaw had a moment of indecision — should he take the pills? They could be lethally doctored for all he knew. On the other hand, Baker could kill him in a variety of ways, and would surely not bother with such a pedestrian solution.

He could do with ridding himself of the last traces of the headache, and he suspected that not accepting the pills would not make him popular. Conquering his hesitations, he took the pills and drained the glass. Setting it down, he looked back at Baker, trying to return the intent stare he was getting.

'I've been watching you for days, Shaw, and I can't make my mind up about you. You could be an innocent, a sucker roped in by your friend, or you could be the one I need to look out for.' Baker leaned back in his chair. 'Ryland must have told you that I want someone to act for me with Dave Damerell. Just to cover my back if he's spitting mad about Harry. I don't want Damerell gutting me on sight. I'm sure that he'd want in on this deal, though.

'If Ryland takes a sample of the goods over to England and tells Damerell that I can get a steady supply for him, we can all get on with what we do best. Everyone rakes in the money. How does that sound to you?'

Shaw waited for a long moment before answering. 'It sounds like throwing meat to the wolf following your sleigh, but if Damerell was the wolf, I'd do the same,' he said wryly. 'What you would get from the arrangement is obvious, but what would *we* get if we agree to do this?'

'*We?* So you *are* working with Ryland?'

'At the moment, I'll admit that you have the upper hand, Baker, so it does me no favours to lie. Ryland brought me on board once he had met Damerell several months ago. I travel widely as part of my work, and he knew about some experiences I've had that opened my eyes to the opportunities out there.'

Shaw looked meaningfully round the room, lingering on a set of ivory figures. 'I know a bit about what can and can't be brought into this country, and how to get things if you want them badly enough. I can see a few bits and pieces here that I'd bet never went through customs.' He returned his gaze to Baker and shifted his weight more comfortably in his chair. 'Ben had a half-baked idea about setting Damerell up, or double-crossing him somehow. He was a fool to consider it. From what I've heard, you know better than that.'

'No point grabbing something you can't hold on to,' Baker agreed. 'Harry didn't realise that either.'

'It sounds like Scadden did too much grabbing all round,' Shaw said, glancing towards Melanie who was watching them silently from where she leaned against the counter. She still held the gun, although it was no longer trained on Shaw. Her face betrayed nothing, but the line of Baker's jaw tightened.

'He's out of the picture now,' Baker said decisively.

'You know, that really threw us,' Shaw said, warming to his role. 'For a while we were going to call the whole thing off, but I didn't want to waste all the time we'd spent on this.

'Damerell was not at all happy to find someone had already killed his target — you're right to be wary of him. He'd planned to make an example of Scadden, big time. My instinct would be to leave him alone to calm down. So if we act as your go-betweens, it needs to be worth our while. After all, the difference our intervention could make for you is that you should end up rich rather than dead.'

Baker was beginning to look angry, and Shaw wondered if he had pushed him too far, but he and Ryland had agreed that Baker would be suspicious of anything but self-interest in their actions. If they just appeared eager to get away from their prison, the plan might not work.

'*Baker detests weakness,*' Ryland had said. '*We'll get a better chance if you come over as arrogant. It's no good me trying it, he's got my number already.*'

'*What do you mean?*' Shaw had asked.

'*I've spent too long being scared, Nick, and these last few days . . . they've been too much for me. I've managed not to say a lot to Baker, but I could tell he was starting to rethink his plan to use me. I can see he despises me, but you're an unknown quantity.'*

Baker had been staring hard at Shaw, deliberating. Suddenly he reached behind him, opening the door of a cupboard. Shaw tensed, not knowing what to expect, but Baker drew out the bag he had taken from Shaw's car and tossed it onto the table.

'Wallet, car keys — it's all in there except the phone, I'll hold on to that a bit longer,' he said brusquely. 'If you'll sort out Damerell for me, you get to leave here alive. I'd say that's worth something, but I'll also give you a five percent cut of the money I'll get for the first shipment. That's my only offer.'

Shaw pretended to consider the deal as if he had any choice in the matter. His heart was beating rapidly, and he could see that Melanie was no longer holding her gun so casually. He was left in no doubt that she would shoot him if he said no. He held his nerve for a while, then slowly nodded. 'All right, it's a deal.'

Baker nodded with satisfaction, then stood abruptly, scraping the legs of his chair along the tiled floor. 'Come here,' he said, walking to the window.

Shaw rose and crossed to join him. Looking out, he saw an expanse of sea below a grassy cliff. Moored a little way out was a fair-sized boat.

'That's the *Venture*. We'll be going out on her later to do the pick-up,' said Baker. 'Then a couple of my guys will take you and Ryland over to England with the samples for Damerell. It'll take all night, but the forecast is good. As long as you get away from him alive, we'll have you back here sometime tomorrow, and you can miraculously 'find' your poor friend who fell down a cliff and has been stuck ever since.' He turned back to face Shaw.

'Until tonight, I'm going to keep you both here. Don't want you wandering off anywhere.' He was close enough for Shaw to feel intimidated, as was surely Baker's intention.

'Fine, but I'm not staying in that hole,' Shaw replied.

Baker agreed, and shortly afterwards, Shaw and Ryland were installed in a bedroom overlooking the sea. Uncertain whether they could be overheard, Shaw had to stay in character as he explained the deal. Ryland had taken it all in, and had visibly paled when he realised that they would be taken straight on to Damerell, but there was nothing else to do except go along with it and hope for a chance to get the upper hand at some point.

Shaw privately thought their best opportunity would be during the long journey across the Channel, which he guessed would take over five hours at least, even with a fast boat. There was little to be gained by talking when they could not speak freely, so Ryland lay down on the bed and was quickly asleep.

Shaw stayed up, looking out of the window and worriedly going over different plans in his head, but none struck him as being brilliant. Eventually, tiredness overcame him, and he too dozed off.

★　★　★

A fresh breeze blew across the sea and into the cabin of Baker's motor boat.

Baker kept an eye on Shaw and Ryland while it was still light, and left Melanie piloting the boat.

As night fell, Baker had gone up to look out for the supplier's boat, and they had more privacy. The temperature fell as the sun set, and Shaw was hoping that the two things combined might help Ryland to perk up. They had been confined to the cabin and would stay there until the boat reached the rendezvous.

Ryland had been very quiet since he had woken up, and had found it hard going getting on to the boat due to the pain in his knee, but Shaw guessed that the psychological impact of their situation was the greater problem. He seemed to have lost the bluster and self-confidence that were so much a part of his character, and was relying on Shaw to find a way out for both of them.

In a way, it was a relief to be able to take the reins, but Shaw was worried that Ryland would not be able to act quickly enough if they did have a chance to get away. He continued to sip at the flask of coffee that they had been given to share.

171

A thought occurred to him.

'Ben, do you have any family, other than your father?'

Ryland looked up. 'Not anyone close these days. There are a couple of cousins that I haven't seen since my mother died. God, I'm glad she's not around to hear about this. At least Dad's too far gone to know.' He laughed bitterly. 'That was the one thing Damerell couldn't threaten me with — exposing me to my family.' He lowered his voice. 'Nick, I'd really like to nail that bastard, and the whole lot of them if possible.'

'Me too, but the first step is to get away from Baker's men,' Shaw agreed. 'How much do you think you can do with that knee?'

'It's pretty bad, but I don't think we'll be running anywhere. There's no point in having a plan, anyway. If we get a chance, we take it. That's all.'

Shaw nodded. There really was not any more to be said. He began to wonder what Louisa was thinking. Would she have raised the alarm yet? Would Rick have contacted her? It was nearing ten o'clock and she would surely be worried about him.

Could Raven even now be adding his name to the list of missing persons, or would interrogating Curzon be taking all his attention?

The engine sound changed, and they could hear Baker and his wife talking, though they could not make out the words.

'Do you have any idea where we are?' Ryland asked, peering out of the small window.

'I can see lights off to the right in the distance, but it doesn't tell me anything. Wait, though. There's a boat coming.' Shaw saw the light moving up and down as the boat got closer.

'That must be the new supplier,' Ryland said tensely. 'Do you think we'll get to see him?'

Shaw did not have time to answer as Baker stuck his head through the doorway and called them up.

It was completely dark by then, and all Shaw could see was their own boat and the new one which was nearly alongside.

There was an indistinct figure in the other boat, which Shaw could see was indeed called the *Ange de la Mer*. It was bigger and sleeker than Baker's boat, and probably faster.

Baker caught a rope thrown from the *Ange de la Mer* and made it fast on a metal hook on his own boat. He started talking to the man in a tone too low for Shaw to make out many words, although he had no difficulty interpreting the meaning. The newcomer was not happy.

'What do you think's going on?' Ryland muttered.

'I'm sure I heard Scadden's name mentioned. I don't think the supplier trusts Baker.'

'If they just leave without making the exchange, where would that leave us?'

'At sea,' Shaw replied curtly.

After a couple of tense minutes, Baker retrieved a small rucksack from beneath the steering wheel. He opened it and took out a tightly-bound wad of money. He stood back a little, keeping the bag firmly out of reach. This time Shaw could hear his words.

'Tell your boss that there's a new set-up on Jersey, but with the same terms. Scadden was getting careless and would have been a liability. I'm not.' Baker tossed the money back into the rucksack. 'I'm not making the exchange until I've spoken with him.'

The other man turned on his heel without another word and disappeared into the cabin for a few moments before returning. 'Come aboard, then.'

Baker nodded and stepped onto the larger boat. He glanced back at Shaw and Ryland, sitting uncomfortably on the narrow seat that ran along the edge of the boat. 'Melanie, you come too, and bring the keys. Those two will be fine here. There's nowhere to go, after all.'

A few moments later Shaw and Ryland were alone on the boat, but painfully aware that they could easily be seen by anyone watching from the *Ange de la Mer*.

'Any ideas?' Ryland asked.

'Short of swimming, no. Wait, is there a radio? We could call for help!' Shaw sat up straighter to look at the instrument panel by the wheel. There was a handset on a cord that must be it. Then he took stock. He had only used a marine radio once before and had no idea about what frequency to send out a distress message on. In all likelihood he would be picked up by the *Ange de la Mer* and whoever her captain was. A hurried conversation with Ryland showed that he was clueless too, and it was only seconds later that the Bakers appeared again.

Baker was looking smug and his wife was smiling for once. He was carrying two large sports bags that presumably contained drugs, which he took below to the small cabin. The line connecting the two boats was undone and he steered the *Venture* away.

'Done it!' he exclaimed fiercely. 'I should've ditched bloody Flash Harry years ago.'

'Haugen will be fine with the arrangement,' Melanie agreed. 'There's no way the police can link you to Harry's death; your alibi won't be broken as long as Fred Milton wants to stay in office.'

Shaw and Ryland exchanged a glance.

Both had heard of Frederick Milton — a leading Senator in local government. If he was in Baker's palm, it was no wonder that George Bisson's information kept on getting ignored.

Baker laughed. 'He's not going to do anything stupid. We're home and dry on that one. Now we just need Damerell on board, and this is where we bring our two guests in.' He looked triumphantly over at Shaw and Ryland.

'All right,' Shaw said, standing up and pushing his fears as far to the back of his mind as he could. 'Show me the merchandise, and brief me about the supplier and how you want this to work.'

'Come down here.' Baker descended to the cabin, leaving Melanie to steer. 'We're going to do a changeover. I'm staying here and you'll be escorted to England by two of my best men. Don't try to cross them, or they will kill one of you, and the other can make the deal. It's the easiest thing possible to lose a body at sea.'

He paused and watched for their reactions.

Ryland merely nodded and Shaw stared back steadily at Baker.

'Okay, so you know where you stand,' Baker continued. 'The supplier's called Alex Haugen and he says he has a small network in Europe at the moment. He doesn't shift large amounts, but he does have the top-quality stuff.'

He proceeded to explain the proposed deal and how Damerell could benefit from it.

Shaw tried to concentrate on Baker's words, although he was finding it difficult. Ryland asked a few questions about the ins and outs of the set-up, reminding Shaw that he did in fact know a lot about smuggling. Listening to him, it crossed his mind that it was Ryland's weakness that had got them into this precarious situation, and he felt his anger returning. *Use it properly*, he told himself. *Use it to save your lives*.

Ryland was not the enemy. The men who used people's weaknesses to make fortunes, who profited from the cycle of crime they perpetuated, were the enemy. He looked closely at Baker, burning the hateful face into his memory. In the silence of his mind he made a promise that he would not stop until he had brought him down, one way or another.

9

The moon had risen, but was at its thinnest: just a sliver of light in the sky, giving hardly any illumination. Ryland had been sunk in a gloomy silence for a while, but he suddenly nudged Shaw. 'Look,' he said softly, glancing meaningfully at the window.

Shaw did so, but could not make much sense of the darkened scene. 'What is it?' he replied.

'I think we're coming in to Fliquet Bay. I recognise that little tower. I guess the handover is going to happen soon.'

Ryland proved to be right, and shortly after that there was a bump as a small boat came alongside. Baker cursorily introduced two of his men, Mark and Nat, who would be his eyes and ears in the meeting with Damerell.

Shaw summed them up as reliable and ruthless, and began to despair of finding a way to escape. He and Ryland were moved up to the open deck and seated on the bench once again, in full view of Nat, who seemed quite capable of killing them if they caused him trouble.

'Mark. Call me when the meeting's over. I want to know the outcome as soon as possible, and so does Haugen,' Baker said.

Then he and Melanie climbed into the dinghy that the others had rowed out in.

Just before he pushed off, he said to Shaw: 'Do your job properly with Damerell and we all come out of this richer. Don't screw it up.'

Shaw did not reply. He just watched until Baker was out of sight

Mark, a tall, sturdily-built man in late middle-age with curly dark grey hair and glasses, moved the *Venture* out of Fliquet Bay, while the much younger Nat kept a close watch on Shaw and Ryland. So much so that he failed to notice the dark shape of a boat that was following them at a distance.

Shaw, facing the back of the boat, did notice, and felt a shiver of hope. He looked at his watch. It was nearly half-past one. Too late for most casual sailors. He watched surreptitiously for minute after minute, and it really did look like they were being followed.

Could it possibly mean that the police or coastguards were on to Baker? He looked away, fearful of drawing attention to the boat, and thought hard.

Surely the authorities would have flashing lights or a loudhailer to pull the *Venture* over. If so, perhaps they were waiting to get closer before declaring their presence. Now he knew the boat was there, it was almost impossible not to let his eyes slide to look at it. He shifted his position and stared down at the door to the cabin instead.

He felt Ryland suddenly tense on the seat next to him, and prayed that Nat had not noticed, but a moment later his heart sank.

'Mark, we've got company!' Nat said tensely. 'A boat about two hundred yards back.'

'Probably nothing, but keep an eye on it,' Mark replied more calmly.

'It's right on course for us.'

'All right. I'll change direction and we'll see what happens.' The boat lurched to one side and then straightened out, heading east.

All four of them watched the following boat continue on its original line, getting further away.

'Nothing to worry about,' Mark said smugly. 'Settle down. It's a long way, and I want you to be on form when it's your turn at the wheel. Why don't you lock these two downstairs? Then you can relax.'

Shaw glanced at Ryland in alarm. They would be completely stuck if that happened. Ryland obviously felt the same, for he made a sudden grab for Nat. He managed to push the startled man off-balance and onto the floor, but Nat was both stronger and uninjured. He quickly heaved Ryland off and punched him hard in the face before Shaw had even started to move.

Ryland's attack had caught Shaw by surprise, and he did not know whether to help Ryland with Nat or go for Mark. Making up his mind, he kicked Nat as hard as he could in the chest and turned to go for Mark, only to find a gun pointed at his face.

'Okay, you've had your little moment now,' Mark said, unruffled by the escape attempt. 'Time to stop messing about. You're stuck with our schedule for now, just accept that.'

He looked at Nat, who was holding his arms tightly across his body and grimacing. 'Has he broken any ribs?'

'It bloody hurts! That's all I can tell right now,' Nat answered angrily.

Mark looked appraisingly at him. 'You take the wheel for a moment.' He beckoned with his gun to Shaw and Ryland. 'Downstairs! Now!'

Ryland could barely walk, as he had fallen heavily when Nat fought back, and Shaw was helping him hobble to the cabin door when the *Venture* was suddenly illuminated by strong light. He looked round and saw something big speeding towards them, its headlights blazing.

Mark finally looked worried. He pushed the throttle to the maximum and the *Venture* surged forward, toppling Ryland and Shaw backwards as it did so.

'Nat! We've got trouble!' he said sharply, but any further commands were cut off as they were rammed.

Shaw was already on the floor, but the force knocked him sideways, and he heard Ryland cry out with pain. Slightly stunned, he struggled to his feet, desperately trying to make sense of events. If it was the police or coastguard, then they would surely not have crashed into them. Whatever the explanation, he had to make use of the distraction.

Glancing quickly around him, he saw Ryland hugging his knee tightly, his face twisted with pain and fear. Nat had got to his feet and was shouting furiously, while Mark was trying to get the *Venture* to move.

Deciding that it was now or never, Shaw leaped on Nat, bringing all his weight to bear. They fell to the deck, and this time Nat was too winded to get up. Leaving his adversary wheezing hopelessly, Shaw turned his attention to Mark, half-expecting to be shot at any moment

— but the older man had troubles of his own.

Someone from the other boat had clambered aboard the *Venture*, and currently had his hand clamped around Mark's wrist, trying to get the gun away from him. There was a deafening report as the gun went off, but the bullet only hit the water; and with a final wrench, the newcomer grabbed the gun and dropped it overboard.

'Are you all right, Nick?' the man said, finally turning round.

'Christian!' Shaw exclaimed, recognising the German at last. 'How . . . ? What are you doing here?' His brain was spinning with relief and confusion.

'Can we put these two somewhere out of the way first?' Beck answered. He was breathing heavily and watching the two smugglers like a hawk. 'Give me a hand to get them down into the cabin.'

Mark and Nat seemed to have had the fight knocked out of them, at least for the moment, and it did not prove difficult to lock them up.

When they were secure, Beck called

out: 'Harry, tie us together and come over, will you?' He looked worriedly at Ryland. 'You don't look too good. Are you Ben?'

Ryland was sweating and looked grey, but he nodded. 'It's my knee. I think it's broken this time.'

'Okay, we'd better get you round to St Helier. At this time of night I don't think we'd get a taxi out to Fliquet Bay, even though it's nearer to us. What about you, Nick, any injuries?'

'I'm fine,' Shaw answered, the tension beginning to leave him now that the immediate danger had passed. 'I just can't understand how on earth you turned up out here!'

'Luck!' Beck grinned. 'I bumped into an old friend, Harry Johnson, and we were trying to beat his fastest time from Jersey to France. He's got a wonderful boat, *Siren Song*, and we were flying when he spotted this, right in our way. You don't get many people out at this time of night, and I was curious enough to get his binoculars out. It was then that I recognised you. It didn't look like you were pleased to be there, and I remembered our conversation about Ben, so I thought we should investigate.'

'Thank God you did!' Shaw quickly explained the events of the last day.

Johnson, who was a young man with dark red hair, was looking over the controls of the boat while Beck listened attentively to the tale.

'You've had a narrow escape, my friends. It sounds like we got here just in time.'

'But what do we do now?' Shaw asked, worry starting to return as the initial euphoria wore off. 'Do we leave the *Venture* adrift and tell the police when we get Ben to hospital?'

'Why do you think boats carry radios?' Beck asked. 'Harry can call the coastguard and give them the position, and we'll head off.'

He paused, drumming his fingers absentmindedly on the side of the boat. 'Although that could be a bit risky. If anything went wrong and the smugglers' boat sank, they'd drown. I've a better idea. Nick, why don't you take the *Siren*

Song back to St Helier? You said you'd done some sailing before.'

'Well . . . yes, but not for a few years, and never at night,' Shaw answered, unsure whether he would be up to it. 'I wouldn't want to damage the boat.'

'Don't worry about that. It's fully insured,' Johnson said. He looked at Beck speculatively. 'Were you thinking that we should take this boat, the *Venture*, and those two smugglers in ourselves, make sure that they don't get away?'

'Exactly!' Beck said, his eyes gleaming with excitement. 'That way, Nick can get his friend to hospital as soon as possible, and you and I can bring this boat in more slowly, in case of damage. I'll radio ahead to the coastguard.' He chuckled. 'Imagine the scene: two smugglers and their drugs to boot, with us as the captors waiting triumphantly when the police finally catch up.'

'No,' Ryland broke in flatly. 'We should just leave them. Call the police and leave them here. It's too dangerous to do anything else.' He spoke with feeling. 'I underestimated these kind of people once, and I'm not going to do it again. We're safe, and with the drugs and our witness evidence, the police will have what they need.'

'I agree with Ben,' Shaw said. Beck was just the same sort as Ryland used to be — impetuous, overconfident, and with a leaning towards excitement. 'It's not worth the risk.'

Beck looked at the two exhausted men and then exchanged a glance with Johnson. He ran his fingers through his short fair hair.

'You've had a truly bad time of it, and it's making you more anxious than you need to be. I still think we can't abandon Baker's men to the possibility of drowning. Their boat took quite a bash, and even the smallest hole can sink a ship given time.'

'God.' Shaw sighed. 'Well I suppose I wouldn't want them to die, and I do want to get Ben ashore, but what if they get out?'

'They won't. And anyway, there's two of us,' Beck replied, exasperation with Shaw and Ryland's caution starting to make his easy-going nature fray.

'Look, we really need to make a decision,' Johnson interjected. He looked around at each of them and his eyes rested on Beck.

'He's right, you know, you do take too many chances. It would be far easier to leave them here,' he said, with a slight emphasis in his voice. 'Have you really thought this through?'

Beck returned the questioning stare with a steady gaze of his own. 'Trust me. This will work out.'

Johnson appeared unconvinced, but he turned away with a shrug. 'Well, if you're certain you know what you're doing, we'd better carry Ben onto the *Siren*.'

Shaw gave in. Ryland tried to argue the point further, but the pain from his knee was dreadful, and he could not resist the combined efforts of all three men. Beck and Johnson chose to do the lifting, and swiftly had him installed on the *Siren Song*. Johnson quickly ran through the controls with Shaw, who was relieved to find that it was very like the boats he had used in the past. While he listened to the instructions, he could not shake a niggling feeling that he was missing something.

It was like an itch at the back of his head, but he was tired and stressed and he pushed the sensation away. He would work out what it was once they were safely ashore.

' . . . afraid it's not working, but you shouldn't need to use it, we'll be just behind you,' Johnson was saying.

Shaw shook his head, trying to clear it. 'Sorry, what were you saying?'

'The radio, it's dead. Must have taken a knock when we rammed the *Venture*.' Johnson picked up a rucksack from beneath the steering wheel. 'Just take it easy and you'll be in St Helier in no time.' Light-footed, he jumped on board the *Venture* and untied the two boats.

'See you soon, Nick,' called Beck. 'We'll be a few minutes getting ready. You set off now.'

Raising his hand in acknowledgement, Shaw turned the engine on, and swung the *Siren Song* away from the *Venture*. Now that the immediate danger had passed, he was seriously flagging. The adrenaline was draining away and revealing the exhaustion underneath.

At least all he had to do was steer an easy course, keeping the land at a constant distance until they reached the harbour. Peering across the water, briefly illuminated by the boat's lights, he knew he had to stay awake, but every part of him ached with tiredness.

Ryland was finding talking tiring, so Shaw did not want to put pressure on him by chatting; and besides, he could not think of what to say.

Gritting his teeth, he ran over things in his head, promising himself that he would be able to sleep soon enough.

Shaw did not know how long it was before he realised that he could not see the *Venture* behind them. He had not bothered to look back, but when he turned to check on Ryland he saw that the sea was dark on all sides. Doubts took hold of him. Should he wait until they caught up? What if there had been a problem? Should he go back and find them? He felt the stress mounting again.

He had to get Ben to a hospital, but if Mark and Nat had somehow overpowered Beck and Johnson, they were in real danger. He slowed the *Siren Song*, trying to work out what to do. His wavering was interrupted by the sound of a powerful boat approaching.

To his surprise, however, it was not the *Venture*. It was coming from the other direction.

A few moments later, the sea was lit up by not one but two new boats. One was unmistakably a police boat with a powerful searchlight on the front, but the other was small and fast.

Shaw cut the engine and turned on the cabin lights before waving his arms at the police boat. The relief that flooded through him was overwhelming. He sat down next to Ryland and barely registered the policeman who swung himself down to the *Siren Song* and started gently checking Ryland's leg over.

The police boat then pulled away and set off again, leaving room for the other boat which had also pulled up.

Shaw watched it without much curiosity at first, but when he saw a familiar figure emerge from behind the wheel, his face broke into a tired smile. 'George! So you got in at the kill after all? Baker and his team are going down for sure this time. The *Venture*'s back there somewhere with all the evidence you could wish for.'

Bisson shook his head. 'It's not as simple as that. For one, we'll need to catch it, and they've already got a head start.'

'It's all right. Two guys are bringing it back for you, although they might need some help. I thought they'd be here by now.' Shaw rubbed his forehead. The nagging feeling was back.

'If you mean that German, then I very much doubt it,' Bisson answered with some impatience. 'Raven finally worked it out, with a lot of prodding from me. Christian Beck *is* the new supplier, and right now he's running off with the money *and* the drugs.'

10

The cool night air suddenly felt colder still to Shaw. He looked at Bisson's earnest face, and then at the policeman who was talking reassuringly to the exhausted Ryland.

The man looked up at Shaw and, rightly interpreting his look of incredulity, nodded. 'My colleagues have gone to apprehend Mr Beck, also known as Alex Haugen, for drug running.'

He finished winding a bandage round the damaged knee and sat back on his haunches. 'Detective Chief Inspector Raven is leading the operation. I'm sure he can explain it later. For the moment, my priority is to bring the stolen boat back to shore, and get you two checked over at the hospital.'

'Stolen?' Shaw, his mind reeling, latched onto the word.

'That was what got us out here,' Bisson said, with some satisfaction. 'I was watching the sea as usual, and I saw *Siren Song* heading along the coast. Now, her owner, Sally Humford, never, ever takes her out at night, so I smelled a rat. When I called the police, Raven asked to speak to me, and explained that they had made a breakthrough with that killer they had in custody — Samuel Curzon. Once he decided to make a deal with the police, he came up with all sorts of information, including some suspicions of his own.

'He's been on the island longer than we realised, getting the goods on people for Damerell, and he got very interested when he found out Haugen was here. Apparently he had seen him once before, working for a French supplier a few years ago.'

'Oh, God. So when Beck — I mean, Haugen — started talking to me that night, it wasn't by chance?' Shaw asked, feeling increasingly sick. The German's smiling face as he waved goodbye seemed to hang in front of his eyes and taunt him.

'I don't know the ins and outs, but I guess he was sussing out the situation here on Jersey; and when old Harry

Scadden turned up dead, he saw his chance to tip the balance in his favour.'

Bisson looked at his watch. 'Nick, it's so late it's almost early, and you've had one hell of a night. There's nothing more you can do here. Leave it to the police now.' He looked at the policeman. 'I'll head back home if that's all right, you know where to find me. Take care, you two, and get some sleep.'

It was getting light by the time Shaw was finally able to take Bisson's advice. Judged too well to need a hospital bed, but taken pity on by one of the nurses, he was given a pillow and a blanket and shown to a quiet lounge area with a sofa.

Despite the questions racing through his mind, he slept like a log.

★   ★   ★

It might have been the smell of coffee that woke him, or the unmistakable tang of a bacon sandwich with brown sauce. Whichever it was, Shaw gradually became aware of sunlight streaming in through a window and a gentle buzz of noise as the hospital came to life.

The sofa which had seemed so inviting a few hours before was losing its appeal, and he had a crick in his neck as well as the beginnings of bruises all down one side. He stifled a groan and slowly pushed himself upright, opening his eyes as he did so.

'Finally! I drop everything to get over here, and when I find you, you're sleeping like a baby.' Louisa watched him focus on her and saw the foolish, delighted smile form on his face before she grabbed him in a fierce hug.

Returning the hug with interest, Shaw felt better than he had in days. 'My God, you're a sight for sore eyes . . . and sore legs, chest, and head, to be honest.'

'Don't moan,' Louisa joked. 'The nurse I spoke with said you were just a bit bruised and shaken. I, on the other hand, had hours on the journey to worry that you were dead or being tortured or . . . ' Her voice tailed off and the smile faltered. 'Nick, I've never been so frightened in my life.'

Not knowing what he could say, Shaw just looked at her instead. Her hair was tied back in its usual ponytail, but her clothes were mismatched and her eyes had dark circles under them.

'Thank you for coming,' he finally said, his quiet voice putting a lot of unspoken emotion into the words.

Louisa shifted her eyes from his gaze. 'Anytime,' she answered lightly. 'I think we can go and see Ben in about an hour if you like.'

Shaw raised his eyebrows. 'Not if you're going to lay into him!'

'I wouldn't do that to a man in hospital. In any case, I think he's going to be grilled by DCI Raven and the Devon authorities. He doesn't need me telling him off as well. Though I hope he bloody well grows up after this.'

'I think he probably has,' Shaw said, almost to himself. The memory of Ryland's pain-wracked face was vivid. He stood up gingerly and bounced on the balls of his feet a couple of times. 'I don't feel *too* bad. I want to have some food before I have to talk to anyone.'

'You're talking to me,' Louisa pointed out.

'Yes, but you're different,' Shaw said affectionately, and they set off to find the cafeteria.

Halfway through a fry-up which they decided was far too fat-laden to be served in a hospital, Louisa's phone rang. After a few words, she turned to Shaw. 'The Detective Inspector would like to meet us here. He needs to take a statement from you and Ben.'

'Did they get Haugen?' Shaw asked eagerly.

'Yes, but he says he'll tell you the details later,' Louisa replied. 'He'll meet us at the front of the hospital in ten minutes.'

True to his word, Raven was waiting at the entrance for them. 'Mr Shaw, Detective Sergeant West,' he greeted them. 'How are you?'

'Okay, but desperate for explanations,' Shaw answered. He noticed that Raven did not look as relieved as he would have expected.

'I would be too. I'll need you to give a

formal statement as well, but can you tell me what's been happening during the last twenty-four hours? Then I promise to tell you what I can. There's a room we can use in the hospital.'

Shaw agreed, and they went back inside to a small room only just bigger than a broom cupboard. He went over all that had happened after he left to explore the north of the island. Raven asked question after question, sifting through the information carefully. When they reached the point where Haugen and his friend appeared, Shaw broke off his narrative.

'Who was Harry Johnson?' he asked. 'I take it he was in on all this?'

'Yes, he was indeed. Johnson — and that *is* his real name — seems to have been working with Haugen for a couple of years, and this was a joint venture of theirs. He was none too happy when we caught up with them. Turned on Haugen violently. He was of the opinion that if they had simply killed you all, they would have been home free.'

'That kind of makes sense,' Shaw admitted. 'I don't understand why they bothered to rescue us in the first place, or how it all fits together. If Haugen was the supplier Baker was so desperate to get in with, why did he suddenly change his mind and double-cross Baker?'

'From what we've pieced together, I believe that Haugen was winging it most of the time. Johnson talked a lot last night, and he claimed that they only had one consignment of drugs left to sell, not a regular supply. When Scadden wanted to set up his own deal, Haugen had no way to follow through on his promises. He's a chancer; in fact, I'd call him unstable. He had originally planned to fob off Scadden — or Baker, as it turned out — with a bag that he would switch at the last minute. Then they would be off with the money and the drugs, ready to try the con somewhere else, far away from Jersey.'

'That's stupidly dangerous!' Louisa exclaimed. 'Did they really think it would work?'

'Johnson didn't. He flatly refused, so they carried through the first part of the plan, taking the money for the real drugs.

It was when Haugen spotted Mr Shaw and Mr Ryland on Baker's boat that he decided to follow and see if an opportunity presented itself. Johnson had stolen the *Siren Song* earlier that evening, as they planned to go their separate ways after the handover. Haugen convinced him that they had a chance to keep both the money and the drugs, and they followed at a distance.

'When Baker went ashore, he decided they would stage a rescue, reckoning that if the police subsequently tried to find out where the *Venture* had gone, you would be available to suggest that Haugen and Johnson must have either sunk or been attacked.'

'But that would still leave Baker's men, Mark and Nat. Were they going to bribe them or something?' Shaw asked.

Raven paused and changed position in his chair. 'You said that when you and Mr Ryland left the *Venture*, Mark and Nat were locked in the cabin, is that right?'

Shaw nodded.

'We didn't get there in time.' Raven looked sombre. 'Both men had already been shot dead, probably as soon as you were far enough away not to hear.'

Listening to Raven's words, Shaw felt a numbness seeping into him. He tried to speak, but his throat would not work and he coughed instead.

Louisa's hand found his and she said something, but for a moment he did not hear her.

'Nick, we can stop for a bit if you want,' she repeated quietly.

Shaw found he had been staring blankly at the table, and he roused himself. 'No, I want . . . is there much left of the story?' he managed to say.

'Not really. Johnson gave up as soon as he saw our boat. Haugen tried to jump overboard and swim to shore, but we hauled him out. He's clammed up now. Won't say a thing until his lawyer arrives. It doesn't really matter when Johnson is spilling out his life history in the next room. He's been in trouble before, and he's decided the best way to shorten his sentence is to plead guilty and tell the public prosecutor everything he knows.'

Raven looked at Shaw with concern.

'I'm sorry it took us so long to get to you. It was George Bisson who gave us the final piece of information.'

'When he told you about the *Siren Song* being stolen?' Shaw asked.

'Actually, no. It was when he called me to report the pushy German man who had come round asking him about smuggling,' Raven replied with a wry smile.

'What?' Shaw exclaimed. 'Haugen went to his house?'

'It seems that Haugen claimed you had sent him, and asked Bisson to go over everything he knew about the smuggling that went on around Jersey. Bisson didn't like the look of him, and got rid of him pretty quickly. Then he called me. When we added together his suspicions with Curzon's memory of seeing Haugen before, we knew we were on to something.'

'Well, it was Larry Baker who had Ben all that time. Why didn't you check there?' Louisa asked. Her tone was polite but Shaw could feel trouble brewing.

'We did,' Raven answered. 'I had

someone watching the house for a day, but there was no suspicious behaviour. I'll admit that I was very surprised when Baker turned out to be responsible for both the abductions and Scadden's murder. I honestly thought he wasn't cut out for it.'

'Have we finished for the moment?' Louisa asked abruptly. 'I think Nick would like to see Ben.'

From the angle of her chin and from long experience, Shaw knew she was getting angry about Raven's failure to properly consider Baker. Rather than have her lose her temper with a superior officer, he quickly backed her up. In any case, he needed a bit of time to take in just how dangerous Haugen and Johnson really were. His mind kept conjuring up an image of Mark and Nat, lying in the cabin with bullet holes through their heads.

Raven readily agreed and accompanied them to the room Ben had been given.

Shaw stopped just outside it as a thought struck him. 'Have you arrested the Bakers?' he asked.

'I hadn't got to that part yet,' Raven answered with a glance at Louisa. 'We picked them up in the early hours of the morning, and although they're protesting their innocence, it was plain to see that someone had been staying in that cellar room of theirs. We also found some personal items that you and Mr Ryland can have back at some point.' He opened the door of the room and they all entered.

Ryland was still asleep. Even with the summer tan, his face was pale, and he looked utterly drained by his experiences. Louisa's stern expression softened and she let out a long breath. The covers were raised by a cage which kept them from putting pressure on his knee, and there were several wires and tubes trailing in and out of him.

A nurse walked over to the door. 'You can have a quick word, but the doctor wants him to rest as much as possible today.'

'We won't be long,' Raven assured her.

'Ben. It's Nick and Louisa,' Shaw said, hovering awkwardly by the bed.

Ryland slowly came to and opened his

eyes. Looking at them, he started to apologise.

Louisa cut him short. 'Don't worry about that for the moment, Ben. You were stupid and foolhardy, you should have trusted your friends, and you nearly got yourself killed.' She sighed. 'Just don't do it again, all right?'

'No danger of that,' Ryland answered wearily. His eyes moved to look at Raven. 'You don't look like a doctor; you must be the police.'

'Detective Chief Inspector Raven; we did meet a few days ago. I'll need to take a formal statement from you at some point, but not immediately.'

'Okay. I'm not going anywhere for a while.'

'What's the verdict on your knee?' Shaw asked. 'Is it broken?'

'Fractured,' Ryland confirmed with a grimace. 'It'll need surgery.' He looked back at Raven. 'I'll go over everything with you whenever you want. I'm not going to get it wrong this time, whatever happens.'

'It should work out all right, Ben,'

Louisa said. 'You were acting under duress, and your evidence will be vital.' She took his hand and held it for a moment. 'Time to face your responsibilities, but you won't be alone.'

'See, I said you should have told her everything from the start,' Shaw said wryly.

The nurse opened the door. 'I think that's long enough for now, but you could come back during visiting hours.' She regarded Raven with some annoyance. 'Though I expect you'll be allowed back sooner,' she said with ill-concealed disapproval.

They all left the room and found their way out of the hospital.

'Can you come by the station this afternoon for that statement?' Raven asked.

'Of course, but I'll be glad of a few hours' peace and quiet,' Shaw answered.

'Then I'll be going; there's a huge pile of paperwork to do for this case.' Raven took his leave.

Shaw turned to Louisa. 'Am I still booked into the *Pomme d'Or*?'

'No. They've got a conference on. It starts today. Detective Chief Inspector Raven arranged for all your belongings to be packed up, and I've booked us a room at a hotel in St Brelade's Bay for a couple of nights.'

'That's a thing. How did you get the time off to come over here?'

'Don't be an idiot! They *will* give people leave if their nearest and dearest are held captive. After I got in touch with Raven to say that I thought you were missing too, he spoke to my boss. I'll need to go back soon, but we should be okay for a night or two.'

'Then let's get over to the hotel; I'm in desperate need of a bath and a change of clothes.'

'You finally noticed! I was going to have to say something.' Louisa took hold of his hand. 'Right, you're the travel writer — where's the nearest taxi rank?'

*   *   *

The view from their window was wonderful: miles of sand that started

211

almost below their balcony and spread out to join the sea in the distance. The beauty of the island was coming to the fore once more, and he hoped that his memories of it would include enough of the good moments to outweigh the nightmarish ones. He certainly could not blame the lovely coastline for the use people sometimes put it to.

Louisa had been on the phone to his mother and father, putting their minds at ease. He would speak to them himself later on, but knew that it would mean reopening wounds he wanted to leave a little longer. The interview with the police would not be so bad, they would just want the facts; but with his parents, it would be impossible not to mention how gruelling it had been. He was not ready for that yet.

After lunch, Shaw felt revived enough to get his statement taken, and went painstakingly through it all with Raven and an assistant. Most of it was covering old ground, but as he talked, he found it started to make more sense to him.

Each person had been looking to their

own ends, whether driven by greed, vengeance, or a warped sense of adventure. He still found the revelation of Haugen's duplicity shocking. He had been so sure of the good-natured man, perhaps because he reminded him of Ryland. But Ryland would not break the law for the thrill of it, and he would never kill anyone. He had just been immature and got in over his head.

If Louisa was right, Ryland would get off without a custodial sentence, and she had reassured him that there would be protection good enough to keep him safe through the trial and, if necessary, beyond.

After all the papers had been checked and signed, Raven said that they could go. There would be a trial to come back for, maybe several, but that would take months. Leaving the police station with relief, Shaw looked up at the pale blue sky. When he had been stuck in Baker's cellar he had wondered whether he would ever see it again.

They walked aimlessly to begin with, Louisa taking her cue from Shaw, but he found he was subconsciously heading for the street where Harland had died. Veering away from it, they stopped outside a small souvenir shop.

There was a pile of newspapers on display in the window, and he was glad to see that the events of the previous night had not yet hit the stands.

'Louisa?' Shaw finally broke the companionable silence.

'Yes?'

'Did you get to meet George Bisson?'

'No. I arrived too late to see anyone but you. I'd like to, though, if you would.'

'It's really down to him that the police found us. I'd like to thank him.'

A taxi set them down a few yards from Bisson's front door and Shaw knocked on it.

Bisson answered and welcomed them into the living room. 'You're looking a lot better than when I last saw you. How's Ben?'

'It's going to take more than a few hours' sleep to sort him out, his knee got fractured,' Shaw answered. He sank down onto the sofa gratefully. If he were honest, *he* needed more recovery time as well. Most of all, he needed to go home. At least it helped to be in Bisson's comfortable cottage, with a cup of tea, a packet of biscuits, and in the company of people who understood what he had been through.

Louisa had picked up Bisson's copy of the *Jersey Evening Post*. 'The reporters will be round here soon, I expect. I'd advise you to avoid them entirely. You don't want to jeopardise the trials.'

'Definitely not!' Bisson agreed fervently. 'They should all be put away for a long time. Drug trafficking and kidnap carry long sentences. It was a very good haul, and I expect Raven will get the names of some of the others in Baker's gang.'

Shaw and Louisa exchanged a look. He raised his eyebrow and she gave a tiny shrug.

Louisa cleared her throat. 'It'll be in the papers soon enough, Nick.' She turned to Bisson. 'I'm afraid there was more to it than that, by the end. DCI Raven and his men did manage to catch

Haugen and Johnson, that's his accomplice, but not before they had killed the two of Baker's men who had been heading for England.'

'Killed?' Bisson echoed incredulously.

'Either Haugen or Johnson shot them both. There was a young man called Nat and an older one called Mark. Did you know them?' Shaw said.

'Oh Lord,' Bisson sighed. 'That must have been Nat Burren and Mark Fletcher. Yes, I knew them. Mark used to have a fishing boat in the harbour, and Nat helped him out. I'd wondered about those two a couple of times. They never landed enough fish to make the kind of money they were spending, especially Nat. I didn't like them, but they didn't deserve that, no one does.'

'So there were four murders in the end,' Louisa reflected, counting them off on her fingers. 'Harry Scadden, Dominic Harland, Mark Fletcher and Nathaniel Burren.'

'None of them a great loss to the community, but I'd far rather they were behind bars than dead,' Bisson said. He looked out of his window at the view of St Catherine's Bay. 'Well, I don't think I'll be hanging up my binoculars just yet, but a few nights off won't hurt.'

'You think there'll be more smugglers, then?' Shaw asked.

'Inevitably.' Bisson nodded his head in affirmation. 'But if I spot any more, at least the police are going to take more notice of me.' He set his empty teacup down on a table. 'I'm just sorry that you and Ben got mixed up in this. I had no idea it would be so dangerous.'

'I don't think Ben really grasped it either, not until it was too late. But if you hadn't told the police exactly where to find us, we could have been dead, too.'

'I still don't understand why you're not,' Louisa said, her eyes clouded in thought. Rousing herself at the shocked looks from the other two, she quickly clarified her musings. 'I mean, if Haugen was quite all right with killing two men, why not four? It was quite a risk to take.'

'Johnson must have thought so too, from some of the things he said,' Shaw agreed. He thought back over his time spent with Haugen. 'I think Haugen must be a bit delusional. It's almost like he was playing at being a drug smuggler, but also fancied playing hero for a while. Shooting two 'bad guys' was okay, but Ben and I were innocents. It wouldn't have been . . . sporting, if that makes sense.'

'Well, it's going to be interesting to see what comes out at his trial,' Louisa said, getting to her feet. 'We should be on our way, Nick. I want to see Ben, make sure he's on the ball about getting legal representation, and you need to get an early night.'

'That's for sure,' Shaw agreed, wincing as he stood up. His bruises were developing apace. 'Goodbye for now, George. Raven said that we can go home now, and I think we can get a flight tomorrow. I've had enough of sea travel for the moment.'

Bisson bade them goodbye and they stepped out into the balmy afternoon. They joined the small groups of people strolling along the breakwater and walked to the very end.

The view looking back to the shore was

218

stunning and they just stood for a while. Then Louisa spoke. 'You know how, when you met me, you were a little worried by my profession?'

'The whole dealing with criminals and putting your life at risk thing?' Shaw answered, starting to smile as he saw where this was going.

'That's what I mean, yes. Well, I think you may have proved that your job is by far the more dangerous. After all, I spent the last week chained to a desk, not locked in a cellar.'

'It was only for a few hours!' Shaw protested, grinning. 'And I don't intend to make a habit of it.'

'Even so, maybe on the flight back we can think of some rather more sedate occupations you could take up. Like firefighter.'

'Or mercenary,' Shaw said, taking her hand and starting to walk back.

'Or crocodile wrestler!'

'I quite fancy that, we could move to Australia.'

'Have you *seen* the spiders they have there?' Louisa shuddered and laughed.

'Okay, you can stick with travel writing for now.'

'If you like ... but I'll keep the crocodiles in reserve.'

We do hope that you have enjoyed reading this large print book.

Did you know that all of our titles are available for purchase?

We publish a wide range of high quality large print books including:
**Romances, Mysteries, Classics
General Fiction
Non Fiction and Westerns**

Special interest titles available in large print are:
**The Little Oxford Dictionary
Music Book, Song Book
Hymn Book, Service Book**

Also available from us courtesy of Oxford University Press:
**Young Readers' Dictionary
(large print edition)
Young Readers' Thesaurus
(large print edition)**

For further information or a free brochure, please contact us at:
**Ulverscroft Large Print Books Ltd.,
The Green, Bradgate Road, Anstey,
Leicester, LE7 7FU, England.
Tel:** (00 44) **0116 236 4325
Fax:** (00 44) **0116 234 0205**

Other titles in the
Linford Mystery Library:

THE SEPIA SIREN KILLER

Richard A. Lupoff

Prior to World War II, black actors were restricted to minor roles in mainstream films — though there was a 'black' Hollywood that created films with all-black casts for exhibition to black audiences. When a cache of long-lost films is discovered by cinema researchers, the aged director Edward 'Speedy' MacReedy appears to reclaim his place in film history. But insurance investigator Hobart Lindsey and homicide officer Marvia Plum soon find themselves enmeshed in a frightening web of arson and murder with its roots deep in the tragic events of a past era . . .

KILLING COUSINS

Fletcher Flora

Suburban housewife Willie Hogan is selfish, bored, and beautiful, passing her time at the country club and having casual affairs. Her husband Howard doesn't seem to care particularly — until one night she comes home from a party to discover he has packed his things and intends to leave her for good. Panicked, Willie grabs Howard's gun and shoots him dead. With the help of her current paramour, Howard's clever cousin Quincy, the body is disposed of — but unbeknownst to either of them, their problems are only just beginning . . .

A CORNISH VENGEANCE

Rena George

Silas Venning, millionaire owner of a luxury yacht company, is found hanged in a remote Cornish wood. It looks like suicide — but his widow, celebrated artist Laura Anstey, doesn't think so. She enlists Loveday Ross to help prove her suspicions. But there can be no doubts about the killing of Venning's former employee Brian Penrose — not when he's mown down by a hit-and-run driver right in front of Loveday's boyfriend, DI Sam Kitto. Could they be dealing with *two* murders?

THE COVER GIRL KILLER

Richard A. Lupoff

When a chartered helicopter plunges into the icy waters of Lake Tahoe, killing its millionaire passenger, what seems a routine claim against a life insurance policy turns into a complex mystery for investigator Hobart Lindsey and his policewoman girlfriend Marvia Plum — for the multimillion-dollar policy is to go an unnamed model who posed for the cover of an ephemeral mystery paperback in 1951. Lindsey's own life is in danger as he tries to find the now-aged model (if she's still alive!), on a trail full of murder and deception . . .

MURDER DOWN EAST

Victor Rousseau

Rich spinster Abbie Starr dies in her mansion without leaving a will. Her fortune is thought to have been converted into securities that have been hidden in the mansion — but searches there fail to find anything except a big overdraft. The courts give what is left to cousins Jenny Starr and Elsie Garry, allowing them to run the mansion as a boarding house. But when Jenny is found murdered, the evidence points to Elsie as the killer . . .